BRONCOBUSTER!

Other Avalon Books by Kiz Von Robin

THE RELUCTANT GUNFIGHTER

BRONCOBUSTER!

KIZ VON ROBIN

AVALON BOOKS
THOMAS BOUREGY AND COMPANY, INC.
401 LAFAYETTE STREET
NEW YORK, NEW YORK 10003

Library of Congress Catalog Card Number: 89-62148
ISBN 0-8034-8779-7

PRINTED IN THE UNITED STATES OF AMERICA
BY HADDON CRAFTSMEN, SCRANTON, PENNSYLVANIA

To my grandmother, Ruby Wright,
an example and an inspiration

CHAPTER ONE

THE blade of the knife slit a path along one edge of a cowhide, causing a half-inch strip of the tanned latigo to peel off the mother hide and dangle toward the wooden plank flooring. A black and white tomcat stalked the cut strip as it danced tauntingly beyond its claws. As the strip of leather got within reach, the cat pounced, captured it, and rolled over on its back, ripping at an invisible antagonist with its hind legs.

"Here, Cat, stop it."

The voice of Whip Cordeen had a kind but commanding rumble. He reached down to loosen the cat's claws from the strip before its weight cost him a crooked cut with the knife. At that moment, a blue cattle dog leaped through the open doorway to head off the scampering cat, but it leaped over the dog's head to an open windowsill and then leaped out into the sunlight and scaled the outer log wall. The cat reached the roof before the dog realized that it was outside. Then the dog padded out to a spot of shade near the cabin and set up a vigil, hoping to catch the cat when it came down.

Whip held the leather firmly in his strong fingers and pulled the knife through the last inch of hide. He shoved the tanned folds away toward the center of a long table and put the hunting knife back into a sheath on his belt. He rolled the long, thin strip loosely around his open palm while he glanced out the doorway. Locating his partner in the horse corrals, he ambled out into the sunshine.

Ty rode a stout but compact dun mare around the corral at a walk. He turned her slowly, guiding her several times in both directions, and then he kicked the horse out into a jog trot and circled the small, round enclosure. Ty slid the mare to a stop and grinned as he looked at Whip.

"I can't see any reason that this mare was sent up here to us. I won't get no cracked head on this pony."

Ty saw that Whip was watching and listening to him, but the tall man held his tongue, which was normal for Whip Cordeen. Whip could be genial enough when he felt like it, but the problem was, he seldom felt like it. Ty nudged the horse back into motion. Whip was the boss, but they called themselves partners. That way, Whip could leave the socializing to Ty and could ignore the men he chose to ignore simply by saying, "Talk to my partner." Ty watched the mare's ears as he continued to ride her quietly around the corral. He tried to recall Whip's ever saying more than a few sentences at one time, and could remember only a few instances. Oh, well, that was fine, because Ty did enough talking for both of them, and he loved every minute his mouth was at a high lope.

As the dust puffed up, swirling around him and the pudgy mare, Ty observed the mare's ears suddenly pin down snug to her neck for a moment and then abruptly statue themselves at attention, as if looking at some object far off in the timber. He had been here before and knew immediately what was about to unfold, but she caught him half aware and got the jump on him. The mare exploded with a squeal, gained elevation at unbelievable speed, then laid her whole body sideways with the earth. Ty tried to stay with her, but the horse deftly left him on high, clutching for the slapping stirrups. She dropped back to the earth with Ty in uncontrollable but hot pursuit.

He landed hard just inches from her hooves. Somewhere in the dust and the blur of it all, he saw her head snake down toward him with teeth bared. Ty dodged, squirming in the dirt in an attempt to avoid her, but the mare managed to strike him with a forefoot. Ty tried to roll under the bottom pole on the corral fence, but she caught his shirted arm in her teeth and dragged him back into the corral.

Whip dropped the leather strip, grabbed up a stout pole, and vaulted the corral fence. In two strides he reached the mare and laid a heavy swing across the dun beast's foreface and put her stupidly to her knees, half knocked out. The horse forgot about her victim when she found herself the victim, and, having regained her equilibrium, she pivoted on her quarters and retreated to the far side of the corral. After a loud snort, she seemed to change personalities and returned to the sweet, docile mare she had appeared to be at first.

Whip hauled Ty to his feet. He studied the fallen rider briefly, felt the half-grayed cowboy's bitten arm, then made a big deal out of patting the dust off his shirt, as if a dirty cowboy was a thing of pity.

Ty twisted out from under his patting hands and looked around the corral for his hat. He located the dusty crown cover and stomped over to it, grumbling just loud enough for Whip to hear.

"I don't appreciate your pampering. You'd think a feller could get bucked off around here without having to put up with being made fun of. She won't do that again, by cracky."

"We'll sell her," Whip said.

"No, I'm not gonna let her get away with that. I'm gonna ride her!"

"We'll sell her," Whip repeated. And then he strode to the fence without a backward glance at Ty.

Whip was that way—abrupt. Ty wanted to get back on the mare, but Whip was also just as abrupt when he was disobeyed. His name had nothing to do with a whip of any kind, but because he'd whipped every man in the area that cared to tangle with him. Whip didn't go around picking fights, but you didn't scorn him and you didn't dare him.

Ty slowly dusted himself off as he went over to the now-gentle mare. Whip was right, of course. The horse would turn on a human being, and that kind of animal didn't belong in any string where a cowboy's life depended on the good mind of the animal he rode. Ty had liked the mare, but that was all over now, and she'd go down to the horse trader at Magpie Springs.

Whip had firm convictions about the stock he trained into good cow ponies, and he never wasted his time on a killer horse. When excited, they'd return to their original state of mind, no matter how well they were trained. Also, he shot any horse that purposely reared up time after time. That same animal would fall over backward sooner or later, and seldom did a cowboy get another shot at life after that kind of wreck.

Ty unsaddled the mare and turned her loose in one of the corrals. It was nearly noon, and Ty's stomach was a spoiled child. When it kicked and growled, it got fed.

Whip sat inside at a wooden table and munched a biscuit topped with preserves. He put the pan bread in one hand and reached for his coffee cup with the other as Ty's spurs jingled up the porch steps outside the cabin.

Ty had been with him for six years. Though Whip was basically a loner, Ty had just happened along one day and had stayed. Whip had listened in amazement as the man talked almost continuously, not waiting for an answer in order to feed his conversation. Whip didn't like to talk much, and now, after six years of listening to Ty jabber, he doubted he had had to answer more than once or twice a week. This worked fine for both sides, because Ty had trouble keeping a partner since he talked all the time and never let a man get a word in edgewise, and Whip seldom spoke, and therefore the few men with whom he had become acquainted eventually wandered away for lack of company.

"I'm sure a lucky man to get to eat three meals a day," Ty said as he pulled his chair to the table. "By the way, have you talked to Jasper in the last couple of days?"

Whip nodded, and covered another biscuit with preserves. He laid it down and got to his feet. Whip carried the coffeepot to the table and filled both cups, then returned the pot and sat down again.

"Is Jasper sending up more horses soon?" Ty asked. "It seems to me it would be easier to train his horses for a fee instead of buying them outright. Cracky, I sure let that mare sneak up on me today."

Ty stopped to stuff in a biscuit and quickly swig down a couple of mouthfuls of coffee. He picked up a piece of meat left over from breakfast and wolfed it down, then grabbed another biscuit and spooned it over with preserves.

"Saw you dancing with that new schoolmarm down at the spring toe tapper in Magpie Springs. Where'd you learn to dance like that? Ever courted a girl, Whip? Reckon not, you being such a smug reprobate and all. By the way, I heard Jasper was married but his wife won't live out in this godforsaken country. Lives somewhere back East, but I heard she was a beauty. Jasper's riders were telling me that he's expecting his daughter this year. If she comes, will you go and get acquainted with her? I reckon I would if I was as young as you are."

Whip stopped munching and studied Ty. There was no harm in anything his partner had said, but he was beginning to get personal and Whip didn't allow that.

"Change the subject," Whip said, then went back to munching on his biscuit.

Ty nodded, and stuffed in a biscuit and slurped down more coffee. "It'd be smarter if we ran some wild horses instead of risking our necks with these spoiled old cow ponies. I can't figure you sometimes, Whip."

Whip shook his head. "No, and when this isn't smart enough for you, Ty, just let me know. You ain't got no brand on your hip."

"Aw, Whip, don't get sore. I only meant to point out that there's an easier way to earn a dollar. Say, want to go fishing with me after we get done with the horses?"

"No. I'm taking the mare to Magpie Springs, then picking up some supplies."

"You'll be purty late getting in tonight. Why don't you wait until morning?"

While Ty waited for an answer, the blue cattle dog made an entrance at the doorway. He looked back over his shoulder and growled at something outside. The dog's hair stood up over his neck and back. He growled again, lowered his head, and walked stiffly back into the sunlight.

"Heck's taken a dislike to something," Ty mumbled, and he got to his feet and walked to the doorway and looked out. "What in tarnation does he want?" he said sourly. Then he walked to the far wall and took down a carbine from its perch over the fireplace. "Trouble, Whip. Brownie is riding up with a couple of renegades and two men."

Whip got up from his meal and strolled almost casually to his bed at the back of the one-room structure. He removed his gun belt from a peg on the wall near the bed and then strapped on the weapon. He tied the holster down snug to his leg, then slid out the heavy .45 and checked it. He didn't really need to do that, because it was always loaded and cleaned, but he checked it anyway. Whip slid the gun back home and nodded to Ty, indicating that it was time to step out and greet their guests.

The riders were several hundred feet from the cabin when Whip and Ty stepped out. The group called a halt at their appearance, then came on slowly, leading a big blue roan horse between two men. Two Utes rode on each side of a dark, bearded rider on a flashy black horse with silver conchas lightly scattered here and there over the gear.

Whip spoke first: "What's your business, Brownie?"

"Well, Whip, we got a little more horse than we

want, and I hate to shoot a good-looking horse. Heard you were here, so I figured I'd trade him off to you."

"Watch Brownie," Whip whispered as he stepped away from Ty.

Whip motioned the men to lead the blue gelding over closer, then he walked around the horse, examining its legs. It was sound, but its hide was covered with many scars. He returned to the front of the horse and studied its good head, but a smoldering in the dark depths of its eyes told Whip this was an animal to reckon with.

"Where'd he come from?" Whip asked, looking at Brownie.

"Over Kansas way."

"Could a man ride him over into Kansas?"

"I wouldn't recommend it unless the guy wants to swing by the neck."

"What was the brand before it was run?"

"Can't remember at the moment," Brownie answered, then let a sly grin cross his lips. "Doesn't matter, Whip. Either you give me something for him or I put a bullet in his wicked little head right here, and you can put up with his stinking carcass or drag it off yourself."

"Talk to my pardner," Whip said. He walked back to Ty and said in a low tone, "Trade him the dun mare and five dollars. I'll get the money."

"Whip, you don't want that blue piece of hell. He's a bad one and you know it. Besides, he's stolen, and that ain't real healthy."

"I'll give any horse a chance to live. Buy him."

Whip walked back into the cabin and seemed to dismiss Brownie's presence, but once inside, he watched the goings-on out in the yard. Brownie was an outlaw with a reputation for murder, horse stealing, and cattle rustling. He'd done some petty holdups, as gossip had it of late, and how he had managed to elude a noose was anybody's guess.

Whip pulled a rock out of the fireplace, still keeping watch outside, and withdrew ten dollars from his stash, then strolled to the doorway and waited there, leaning against the jamb as he listened to Ty argue with the outlaw.

"That dun mare is a jewel," Ty said. "Why, I just rode her this morning, and I tell you, Brownie, that mare is an angel."

Brownie muttered sourly, "Probably up in the air on wings all the time."

"Of course she can buck, otherwise she wouldn't be here, but that's no problem if you fellers can ride."

"All right," Brownie said, "but you kick in twenty dollars, to boot."

"Cracky, did you get hit on the head?"

"Go where it's hot," Brownie snapped, and drew his .44 from the holster. He leveled the barrel on the blue's head.

Whip walked off the porch as Brownie cocked the pistol. "Put your gun away, Brownie," he said, his lips tight and his voice low.

"Twenty dollars," Brownie repeated, his gun still on the blue.

Whip wrenched the carbine from Ty and leveled the bore on Brownie's waist, jacking in a shell as the carbine came on target. Brownie studied Whip for only a moment, then slowly put his pistol back in the holster.

"Twenty dollars," he said again.

"Ten, and you take it or you're through except for a fast trip to that hot place you were talking about."

Brownie shrugged and turned toward his men. "Put that critter in a corral and catch up the dun mare over there." He looked back at Whip. "You know I won't forget this. Once I kindly chose to overlook, but this is twice now, and I'm beginning to get a little hostile about you pointing a loaded bore at me. I should have shot you last time."

"You pulled the first gun here today," Whip said, and handed the ten dollars to Ty to give to Brownie, all the while keeping the carbine pointed at the outlaw.

A ruckus started in the corral. When the dust had settled, Brownie's men chose to leave the lariat with the blue horse rather than risk their lives getting it off his neck. They caught up the dun mare and returned to Brownie and the two Utes.

The outlaw touched his hat brim and shot a sly grin at Whip that wasn't friendly in the least. "Till next time," he said with a low, wicked laugh, and then he kicked his horse and the outlaw group cantered down off the hillside.

Whip and Ty watched until the gang became little specks in the valley below. Then Whip handed Ty the carbine.

"When did you ever point a gun at Brownie?" Ty asked, scrutinizing his boss. "I saw you two exchanging stares a few years back when that devil first came to this country, but I never heard either of you even speak, let alone you being fool enough to draw down on him. Well, when did you?"

"A long time ago, Ty, and it ain't worth the effort it takes to remember it."

"Well, next time you better shoot first," Ty mumbled. "Otherwise, I'm gonna be missing the best pardner I ever had."

"Does he bother you, Ty?"

"Bother ain't the right word. He scares me to death. He don't like you, Whip, and you've agitated him. I guess you know that Brownie won't face your front and risk getting shot or getting his ears boxed. No, he'll wait behind some big rock and shoot you in the back."

"I know," Whip said quietly, and he gazed off in the direction the outlaw had gone.

Later, Whip leaned on the corral fence and studied the blue roan through the poles. The horse was one in a million, its body perfectly balanced, each part blending pleasingly with the other. In turn, the horse watched Whip, flicking its ears cautiously, waiting for the man to enter the corral. But Whip merely watched, pleased at this action in the horse. The blue would react by what it had learned from the hand of man, not from disposition. Ty came up at that moment.

"Whoopie, pardner, you got a dragon there. Look at his hide. I bet he's eaten a man for every scar, and he's probably thrown a man for every inch of blue hide that ain't scarred up. I tell you, Whip, that's an outlaw."

"Shut up and study him a minute, Ty," Whip said.

Ty did so, glancing off and on at Whip, but once he really looked, he was horseman enough to appreciate the good traits that showed in the blue. The horse was undoubtedly somebody's pride and joy before Brownie latched on to it.

"He's fast and he's strong, but, Whip, you've got your work cut out for you. Don't ask me to ride him. I'd rather not fool with him at all."

"Why, pardner, I don't want this blue horse ruined. After seeing you fall off that fat mare this morning, I won't let you lay a hand on this promising mount."

"Promising? Fell off? Why you badgering, overgrown pair of britches! You just sold her so you wouldn't have to eat crow yourself after you tried to ride her. I'm gonna be laughing till Christmas when you get piled off this promising piece of devil flesh. And by the way, I never ruined a horse in my life!"

Whip watched Ty stomp off toward the saddle

shed. A few minutes later, Ty was sitting outside in the shade repairing his worn tack. Whip turned back toward the corral, where Heck had wandered in and was digging through a pile of manure with his forepaws. Whip wondered at the dog's lack of respect for the horse. Heck was not a dog to get at a disadvantage around stock, but at the moment, he was totally ignoring the big blue gelding that was slowly working his way over to the busy dog. Whip started to whistle to Heck, but saw the dog look up and study the horse, then go back to his business. Whip got really attached to his animals, and felt nervous about Heck's ignoring the horse. One blow from that powerful hoof and Heck would be in dog heaven.

The horse's attitude seemed to change to curiosity. He lowered his muzzle to the dog's back and licked at the dog. At first Heck got uneasy and sniffed the horse's nose. The roan moved in a step closer and flapped his lips gently, making a soft popping noise as he came in contact with the dog's hair. Then the horse's pink tongue slid out and licked at the dog several times. Heck allowed it, though he watched the horse cautiously. Then, as if they'd come to an agreement, Heck went back to his digging. The roan heaved a big sigh, took his weight off one hind leg, and contentedly swished flies.

"Well I'll be doggoned," Whip murmured.

A few minutes later, he had dragged his saddle

out beside Ty and was sitting in the shade of the shed and replacing his saddle strings.

"What were you referring to when you told Brownie the dun mare was a jewel?" Whip asked quietly.

Ty raised his brows and studied Whip a moment. "What makes you so talkative? Are you sick?"

"Jewel?" Whip asked again.

"She *is* a jewel, a diamond in the rough, but real rough. In fact, the roughest piece of horseflesh in the country. I'm kinda hoping she'll roll him around in the air a couple turns, then stomp his hide into the dirt when he lands and chew him like a dog does a bone."

CHAPTER TWO

THE sun hung low in the sky when Whip pulled the saddle off his last horse in the breaking corral. Ty had left for the fishing hole hours ago, hollering at Heck to come along, but the blue dog only followed him a short way, and then trotted back home and lay down in the corral near the blue roan.

Whip hobbled the sweaty bay horse he had just worked, and then turned it loose in the open so that the animal could graze where it needed. He slipped a hackamore over his shoulder and headed for the pen where Heck and the roan were enjoying the lazy afternoon.

Cat tagged along close to his jingling spurs and occasionally took a quick slap at the whirling rowels. Whip reached for the sliding latch to open the gate, but instead lurched forward and almost slammed his face into the heavy closure. He caught himself before he fell against it, and twisted at the same time, trying to see what held his foot down. Cat scrambled off his boot heel just before Whip could grab it. The cat was always attacking something, and when he pounced on Whip's spur, his weight had tripped the unsuspecting cowboy.

Heck fairly exploded from beneath the corral fence, his toenails flinging earth as he converged upon the cat. Cat leaped for a post, tearing out splinters as he clawed his way to the top of the fence. Heck's jaws closed on a mouthful of fur on the end of Cat's tail. The big tom jeered at the dog from his safe position, then meowed at Whip, begging for a pat.

"Don't tempt me, Cat. I don't think you really want me to get my hands on you right this moment. You might lose one of your nine lives."

As Whip opened the gate and stepped inside, the roan horse spooked and bolted across the pen, its tail high like a waving banner. Head flung up, it studied the man from where it had stopped on the far side of the corral. Brownie's lasso strung out behind the horse, still tight about its throat. Whip walked leisurely around the corral until the horse quit spooking at his presence and became more curious than afraid. Soon, Whip was able to get within reach of the dragging lariat. The horse held its ground when he picked up the rope, but when Whip made a slight tug on the rope, it was as if the beast had been poked from behind. The huge blue rapidly closed the gap between them, which made Whip perform some fancy footwork to avoid being trampled. The horse spun with him each time he dodged out of its way. Whip threw a couple feet of slack into a twist behind him, saw the horse step in the twisted snag, and jerked the lariat taut.

The horse went down to his knees but was up in an eye blink, then went down several more times as Whip worked him toward a corral post. The horse managed to get his legs free of the snag, and lunged toward the center of the corral just seconds after Whip got him dallied on the post.

The horse's head jerked down, and the momentum of the leap sent it into a roll and landed it flat against the earth. Immediately, Whip was on its head, trying to press it against the earth, but the blue wasn't through yet.

Whip scrambled out of harm's way as the mighty beast managed to get to his feet, but it got tangled in the rope and flipped itself over backward, falling hard. Just as Whip began to worry that the horse was injured, it came alive, rolling and kicking, until it got to its feet. Once up, the horse stood shakily, trembling from nose to tail.

Whip moved quietly in close to the animal, then worked a caressing hand up the horse's neck to where the lariat choked its windpipe. He removed it and heard the animal's breathing become clear.

He stroked its blue hide several more times, and then walked away from it, grinning at the puzzled expression in its eyes. He had confused the horse with kindness, and that's exactly what he had intended to do.

Whip called Heck, and the dog followed obediently, but when Whip reached the saddle shed, he saw Heck slipping back toward the corral. Whip shook his head again, baffled at the bond that had so quickly sprung up between the horse and the dog. He'd never seen anything like it, especially with a dog like Heck. The dog had been pounded and chewed by horses since it was a pup, and now it was almost being unfaithful to the hand that fed him and preferred the company of a big blue twenty times his size.

Whip went to the cabin and lit the lamp. He started a fire in the stove, then began to peel potatoes, a gift from a good Irish neighbor down the trail. Whip's life had been pretty void of spuds until he'd moved into the valley about ten miles from the Irishman. When a good heavy workhorse happened upon Whip, he would take the animal to the Irishman. A constant supply of potatoes was worth a constant supply of workhorses for his neighbor.

Suddenly Whip heard horses out in the darkness. He blew out the lantern, then reached up, pulled the carbine down from its pegs, and stepped to the side of the open window. He couldn't make out anything in the darkness, but he heard a thud on the porch, and then saw a horse and rider fade into the night. Hearing a muffled sound, he edged his face carefully around the windowsill to get a better look.

A man pulled himself to his feet, grasped the porch post for support, then crumpled back to the boards. Whip instinctively knew that it was Ty. As he stepped out onto the porch, Ty clutched at him and groaned, then clamped a desperate hold on Whip's arm.

"Brownie said . . . to tell you hi . . . and you're next."

Ty slipped into unconsciousness, and sank away from his partner. Whip cursed under his breath, and he picked up the fallen cowboy and carried him into the cabin. He laid Ty on his bed, lit the lamp, and turned back toward him. He stopped in his tracks, shocked at what he saw. His partner's face was knifed savagely, as if he'd been in hand-to-hand combat with a mountain lion. The cuts were about an inch apart and ran the length of both cheeks, and both eyes were beaten purple.

Whip quickly put on a pan of water and grabbed a bottle of horse liniment and a can of bag balm. He pulled a chair up next to Ty's bed and slowly took a closer look as he placed the medicines on the floor. Further examination found three broken ribs on Ty's right side. Whip looked at Ty's mouth, but the blood there was dried black, probably from a bitten tongue. Whip let out a sigh of relief. He had feared that Ty had a punctured lung. Examining the rest of Ty's body, he grimaced when he saw that both hands were crushed and horribly swollen.

Whip spent the next half hour working over Ty's face. He cleaned the wounds with water, then wiped liniment across each one as Ty drifted in and out of consciousness. Next he rubbed salve into the cuts. He tore up a flour-sack towel and wrapped his partner's face as best he could.

Ty regained consciousness, but a whine escaped from his lips as he tried to breathe.

"Whip?" Ty whispered, trying to turn his head.

"I'm right here, Ty. Don't try to move."

"I didn't cross him. Why'd he jump me?" Ty mumbled.

"Let's not talk now. You're gonna be healing for a long while, and you'll have all the time you need to talk later. Can you down some food?"

Ty nodded slightly.

"I reckon you'd better get used to me feeding you for a while. Your dukes are broke like a bunch of eggshells."

Whip got up and finished peeling the potatoes. While they were boiling, he added some beef and a lot of water. He figured Ty would find it easier to drink as much food as he could, so he intended to cook the potatoes to mush and cover them with beef broth.

The cabin was cloaked in silence, and as the night wore on, Whip realized that he missed Ty's incessant jabbering. He watched his partner's breathing, still worried about the condition of his lungs. Later on he would think of retaliation against Brownie, but he didn't want to deal with it at the moment. The most pressing thing was his partner's recovery.

When supper was ready, he raised Ty to a sitting position and raised the cup of food to his lips. Injured as he was, Ty couldn't suppress short remarks about Whip's nursing abilities, and he stubbornly insisted on trying to support the cup with his broken paws. When Whip saw him balance the cup and do a fairly good job of feeding himself, he was relieved.

Ty requested that Whip leave him sitting up for a while after he finished his second cup of food. Whip obliged and they talked briefly, and then Whip stepped through the door and whistled for Heck. The dog came up on the porch a few moments later, and Whip stepped aside and motioned him inside the cabin. This was an unusual thing, because Whip made his animals stay outside at night. Heck backed up, whining and wanting to obey, but positive that he had not understood his master correctly. Whip motioned him in again, and this time Heck didn't hesitate. However, he dropped his head and curled his stumpy tail as best he could, and tried to look small as he edged into the cabin.

"Why?" Ty inquired softly.

"I like my sleep. Heck will growl if anything goes on outside, or if anyone comes near the cabin."

Whip helped Ty gently to a reclining position, and then he blew out the lamps. Ty listened as Whip undressed and got into bed.

"Whip?"

"What?"

"Don't go after Brownie because of what he done to me. It's a trap." A silence ensued while Ty fought to control the pains in his chest. "He's a cold-blooded killer, Whip. He's too much for you to take on." Ty struggled again, then continued. "I saw him draw down on one of his men. He's a gunslinger, Whip, and you ain't, so promise me you won't go after. . . ." Ty moaned at something he couldn't bear, and passed out again. Moments later his voice resumed in the darkness. "I must've passed out. I didn't hear what you said."

"I didn't say," Whip said.

"Well, I said Brownie's a gunslinger. He's fast, Whip, unbelievably fast."

"I know," Whip said softly.

"Promise me," Ty begged.

"No."

"Aw, Whip," Ty moaned.

"Go to sleep or I'm gonna bunk outside in the shed."

The room was silent for a long while. Whip heard Ty moan in pain several times. He knew Ty was worrying about tomorrow and what he was going to do about Brownie.

"To ease your mind, pardner," Whip said, "I have no intention of taking Brownie's bait."

The cabin was again quiet. Heck walked across the wooden floor and whined at the door. After a moment he went near the stove and lay down.

"Whip?" Ty said.

"What?"

"Thanks for the peace of mind."

Within minutes Whip heard the even cadence of Ty's sleeping breaths. Then he snuggled deeper into the blankets and tried to get to sleep too. But a fiery anger burned inside and grew in intensity as the minutes ticked by. In the wee hours of the morning he finally drifted off.

The sun didn't catch Whip Cordeen in the sack. He rolled out just before dawn and built a fire in the stove. Within minutes the aroma of brewing coffee filled the cabin and awoke Ty. Whip nodded a good morning to the invalid cowboy, then he stepped outside the cabin and went to the cellar for eggs and a slab of pork. Heck hightailed it for the corral, where the blue gelding stood with its head over the fence, looking into the sunrise. On his way back from the cellar, Whip glanced down toward the corral and saw the roan nuzzling the dog's fur, and all the while, Heck's stubby tail was wagging so hard that his hips danced.

Back inside the cabin, Whip immediately set to fixing breakfast.

"Can you handle a hot cup of coffee?" he asked Ty.

"Help me up and I'll figure a way."

Whip crossed the room and sat him up. Ty gritted his teeth and whimpered a couple of times, but he didn't pass out. Whip poured Ty a cup and placed the tin container in his swollen hands, but Ty dropped it over and over, unable to curl his swollen fingers around the hot cup.

"Aw, heck, I have to have my coffee," he moaned.

"Just hold on. We'll figure something out."

Whip set the now-empty cup down on the table and went outside to the woodpile. A few minutes later he returned with a short slab of wood. With his hunting knife, he ran the blade around a large knothole several times and made a hole large enough to hold the tin cup.

"Here, hook each end of this slab between your thumb and first finger. Careful, balance it. Now I'll fill it, and all you have to do is tip it. Enjoy your coffee, pard."

Later in the morning, Whip went out to the corrals with the intention of riding, but he was angry. He had learned long ago that anger clashed with patience, and he'd be better off leaving the stock alone today. He turned the rest of the horses in the corrals loose with hobbles, then set to cutting tall grass with the scythe for the blue roan.

Whip spent the next two days keeping a close eye on Ty. The man became impossible. Whip had never seen such a grumpy, short-tempered man. Twice, Whip had doctored his face, but the last time, Ty had kicked and squalled so much that he passed out from the pain he caused himself. When he came to, Whip was trying to apply the bandage, but Ty wiggled his head, fighting Whip's effort.

"By golly, I won't bandage you, then," Whip said.

"By golly, that just suits me fine," Ty retorted. "And you can stop wasting your horse medicine. I don't need it."

"You're gonna get the salve on those cuts whether you like it or not."

"I'll wipe it off!"

"You do that and I'll tie your arms behind your back."

On the morning of the second day, Ty tried to get up out of bed, but his broken ribs put him back down again, so Whip helped him to his feet.

"Now what?" Whip asked.

"Just get me outdoors to the porch and leave me. I'll yell when I'm ready to come back."

Whip obliged, but Ty made his own way back, and hurt himself to the point of passing out when he tried to lie down.

The morning of the third day, Ty gritted his teeth and managed to get to his feet with no help. Whip knew that his partner was going to be all right when he saw that. The main problem now was his broken hands.

Near noon the fourth day, Whip saw dust in the valley below, and he tensed. He watched it for a while before he realized that there were two groups—the front group of riderless horses and the other of mounted horses. This had to be Jasper's cowboys with the new bunch of spoiled mounts. Whip notified Ty of the visitors, then swung open the big gate on the main corral.

Ten minutes later, six of Jasper Hunt's cowboys drove a herd of fifteen head through the opening. Jasper himself rode up to the fence where Whip sat. He was in his fifties, white haired and full of life.

His cheeks were rosy and his eyes seemed to shine when he talked. Jasper was the kind of man who ripened with age, sort of like good whiskey.

"See you're worked nearly to death," Jasper commented, taking a poke at Whip's nonchalant manner up on the corral poles. "Here, behind my saddle, is a sack of spuds from Irish. Where do you want them— What in the world?"

Jasper was staring past Whip into the corral behind him. Heck lay in the shade of the blue roan's shadow, propped against the horse's front legs. The blue roan was interested in the new horses, but appeared not to be moving because he would disturb Heck's comfort.

Whip grinned and slid down off the fence. He untied the sack from behind Jasper's saddle and slung it across his shoulder.

"Lots of strange things happening around here," Whip said. "Step down and come inside. Ty's had some trouble."

Jasper dismounted quickly and peered into Whip's face. "Horse fall on him?"

"No, Brownie did."

Jasper glowered under his shaggy brows, and he cursed the air purple as they walked toward the cabin. Whip put the spuds down in the cellar, then accompanied Jasper up onto the porch. Just as the rancher came under the roof, Cat decided he was an intruder and leaped down on Jasper's head. Whip grabbed for the cat and managed to get a hold on him, but in the process, Jasper got scratched on both cheeks. As Whip let go of Cat after giving him a shake, Jasper drew his shooting iron and aimed it at the sprinting cat as it scaled the wall.

"He ain't worth a toot and needs to be shot, but that's my decision." Whip grabbed Jasper's gun barrel and shoved it downward.

"I wouldn't put up with that!" Jasper said.

"You ain't me." Whip studied the marks on Jasper's cheeks. "Well, now maybe Ty won't feel so bad. You're dang near cut up in the same place, only his are deeper and there's more of them. He's been knifed bad, Jasper, but don't make out like it's as bad as it is. He's scarred for life, and it's ugly, and Ty is bitter as all get-out."

Jasper nodded at his words, then Whip stepped around Jasper and opened the cabin door. He entered with the rancher right on his heels.

"Here's your old boss, and he looks about like you, Ty. Cat took offense to him."

"If that darn dog was doing his job, we wouldn't have to put up with that cursed cat. Hello, Jasper, ain't this a sinful-looking mess on my face? That blasted Brownie carved me up like a Thanksgiving turkey. I wish somebody would get the marshal in Denver to come out here. Just look at my mug and feast your peepers on these mitts! Broke all to heck I am, and that bloody bandit is prancing around as free as a bird."

Jasper found it hard not to stare for a minute.

Then he looked away, almost nauseated by the atrocity committed on Ty's face.

"My gawd," he whispered. "I'll get the marshal, Ty. This has gone too far."

Whip left them alone, and Jasper seated himself at Ty's bedside. Ty had worked for Jasper before joining Whip, and the friendship between the men was strong. They talked together for a few minutes about Brownie, then the conversation settled on Whip.

"You've known him longer than I have. Didn't he work for you when he first came here?"

"Yep," Jasper answered, "but he busted broncs for me only two years. Then he moved out here and started this setup of his own. That was about ten years ago. I never knew anything about the man before that. He just kinda showed up one day. Why are you asking about him?"

"Well, I thought you might know when he had put a gun on Brownie. When Brownie was here a little less than a week ago, Whip put the carbine on him and Brownie said that was twice that Whip had done it. I think that's what made him so mad, and then he caught me down at the fishing hole and almost killed me, hoping Whip would get all steamed up and come after him. But Whip's too smart for that."

"No, I never heard of Whip even speaking to Brownie in the past. Either it happened out in the brush somewhere where nobody saw, or else before

Whip came here. What was Brownie doing on Whip's spread, anyway?"

"He wanted to get some cash out of a blue gelding he couldn't handle. Whip bought him, but the price was what got the gunplay started. Brownie tried to shoot the horse, and Whip dang near shot him. I could feel it coming, and I think Brownie felt that the chance of that happening was pretty darn good, because he didn't hesitate for a minute when Whip pointed that carbine at him. He just slid his iron back into its holster as if he was used to obeying Whip every day of the week."

"That's strange," Jasper said. "Brownie ain't normally a man intimidated by the open end of a gun barrel." Jasper felt a need to pull his eyes away from Ty's carved-up face, and he let his attention wander around the cabin. "I see Whip's revolver hanging there on the peg. I can't understand a man packing a gun belt around in his saddlebags, slung across his saddle horn and every other unlikely place but on his hip."

"Oh, he strapped it on the day Brownie was here," Ty said.

"I thought you said he pointed the carbine at him."

"He did, but he had that pistol tied down on his leg in a way that made the hair stand up on the back of my neck. I had the carbine, but Whip yanked it out of my hands and put it on Brownie instead of using his .45. I didn't understand that, but that was what he did."

"Well, I'll be," Jasper mumbled. "I've never seen him buckle that gun belt around his hips since the day I first laid eyes on him. I had a feeling he was almost scared of it in a way, not as if he was cowardly, of course, but scared like he might have to shoot somebody and he didn't want to. You say Whip bought the horse from Brownie?"

"Yep, and that's got me worried. The dang bandit told Whip in no uncertain terms that the horse was stolen out of Kansas, but Whip bought the devil, anyway. I tell you, Jasper, that big roan is gonna hurt Whip, but he don't seem to be worried, though I sure am. Hey, Jasper, if there's any time Whip ought to crawl up in the middle of that horse, it's right now, today! If he gets in a jam, there'll be somebody around to shoot that beast before Whip gets killed, or at least there will be somebody here besides me to bury his ignorant carcass, since he's dead set on straightening out that horse's outlook on life. Jasper, make Whip see the common sense of riding that horse today, while you're here!"

Jasper got to his feet and carried the chair back to the table. He pursed his lips for a moment, trying to make a decision, then nodded.

"I can take the time, because I see the necessity of it, but, Ty, one of the most important events in my life is going to unfold this afternoon. My daughter, whom I've never seen, is coming in on the evening stage to Magpie Springs. This is probably gonna run me late meeting her, so I guess that tells you where Whip stands in my book." Jasper opened the door, then looked back at Ty. "If I can talk him into it, I'll have the boys come in and haul you out to the corral if you want."

"No need, Jasper. If I got enough reason, I can tolerate these confounded aches and pains and get around a little bit. I'll make it out to the corral. The problem is these cursed hands. I can't touch one stinkin' thing without them hurting so bad it darn near puts me on my knees. Leave the door open and just wave to me if Whip's gonna ride. I can see the corral from here, and I'll head on down."

Jasper left the door ajar and strolled out into the yard. He saw his cowboys and Whip gathered around the blue roan's corral, so Jasper quickly made his way down. He crowded in beside Whip and peered through the corral poles. The horse was lying down near the opposite side of the corral, and Heck was curled up between the horse's legs next to its belly. Jasper shoved his hat back and shook his head.

"Is that some kind of trick you concocted?" he asked Whip.

"No," Whip drawled. "Heck laid claim to the blue bandit right off. He's dang near swore off chasing the cat."

"If you want me to ride with you to track down Brownie, I'm offering."

"No, I'd be dancing to his fiddle," Whip answered coolly, with anger in his eyes. "That's what he wants."

"Somebody has to even this score."

"I will . . . my way," Whip said.

"Ty begged me to talk you into riding this renegade blue bandit while we're here to pick up the pieces. That's sense, Whip, especially with your partner busted up and unable to help if this big roan tries to eat you."

Whip was quiet for a minute while he stared into the corral. He took a deep breath, then nodded to Jasper. "I wanted more ground time on him, but I think you talk sense. I'll saddle him."

CHAPTER THREE

WHEN Whip entered the corral with his saddle in his hands and the hackamore over his shoulder, the roan horse scrambled to its feet with a snort. One of its hooves caught Heck before he could leap out of harm's way, and the dog yelped and hopped on three legs to the safety beyond the corral fence.

Whip didn't like the audience he had, preferring to work a horse alone and unwatched, but it was necessary. He put down the saddle and caught up the horse, careful not to stand in front of it. Apparently, this had been the horse's main advantage in subduing cowboys in the past, simply running them down because he had the size and weight to make that trick destructively effective.

The horse shot nervous looks at the saddle as they crossed the corral. Then, as they came up to it, he swept his ears down against his neck and held them there, and got a really hateful curl to the edges of his nostrils. A sullen look came into his eyes, but he allowed Whip to place the saddle on his back.

As Whip pulled up the cinch, the horse humped slightly, then bounced lightly on his front legs for a moment. Whip took a few more inches out of the cinch, then snugged down his hat and glanced over his shoulder at Jasper.

"Gonna be a heck of a storm under you, Whip," Jasper mumbled, wagging his head back and forth.

Whip turned the horse slowly from the ground. It heaved upward a few feet, grunting as it bowed its head downward, and it hopped several steps with its weight on its hind quarters.

"My, ain't we spoiled, though," one of Jasper's cowboys taunted good-naturedly. "We get front-row seats to this here event. Maybe you'd be safer if you just duked it out with him instead of trying to get on his back."

Whip glanced from under the edge of his hat brim at the cowboy, who had taken a sound whipping from him once. The cowboy averted his eyes and was silent, not sure whether Whip was taking well to the teasing, and certainly not willing to risk finding out. Whip put his attention back on the horse. He led him a few more steps, hoping that the hump in his back might disappear a little, but that was like hoping for popcorn instead of hailstones.

Whip took a snug hold on the headstall with one hand, and pulled the horse's nose slightly toward him as he mounted. To his surprise, the blue allowed him to mount without even a shiver of its withers. Whip took a short hold, then nudged the roan with his heel, turning him to avoid a forward leap. The blue turned so fluidly that it almost spun. Whip let him have enough slack to straighten out of the spin. That's exactly what the blue wanted to achieve, and he took advantage of Whip's error and fairly broke in two, adding spice to the explosion with a savage grunt.

His front shoulders rose, and the powerful hindquarters propelled the blue beast upward to a frightful elevation. The horse's black head couldn't wrench free of Whip's strong grip on the rope, but it managed to bury its velvet nose between its legs just in front of the girth. Whip skillfully sailed upward with the horse, not losing an inch of seat leather.

The horse hesitated when he reached the top of his mighty thrust from the earth, and then the descent came, fast and straight down to the earth. Whip nearly crumpled on impact, his entire torso threatening to become part of the saddle leather. Both knee joints felt rammed to his hips, and his hips into his shoulders. He was shaken so hard that his head popped when the roan leaped skyward again. Giving the left rope a powerful yank, Whip tried to diminish the upward distance, but the seasoned outlaw roan had it all in hand and went as far as he pleased. Then he floated down again, pounding his twelve hundred pounds into the corral dirt and shaking the ground so thoroughly that the men on the fence winced, totally aware of what the big blue was doing to the rider's insides.

Whip stayed with him as he again rose upward like a whirlwind headed for heaven. Then he tried to jerk the roan's nose sideways on the downward plunge, in order to overcome the effect of the impact. Whip failed in that attempt, took the full force of the jarring impact, and when the next upheaval came, he was half bent over the front of the saddle, his body accordioned in one big cramp. When the blue dropped back down and rocked the surface of Mother Earth again, Whip fell out of the saddle and onto the corral dust, his body unable to take any more abuse on the back of the horse. He lay where he fell, out cold to the world.

The horse stopped immediately. He lowered his head, his neck arched and snaked out like a stud horse. Then he bounced in a hesitant, high-floating trot, as if he had huge springs under each hoof. His tail bannered and his eyes blazed like fire. Bolting back across the corral, he was on Whip before any man on the fence could react.

Jasper yelled and leaped down into the corral, drawing his gun. The other six men were already leaping into the corral to save Whip's life from the fiery blue devil. Ty steadied himself against the poles on the fence and stared helplessly, watching what he had feared.

Suddenly a blue whir knocked Jasper off his feet in its passing and tore into the middle of the corral. The dog leaped onto Whip's back, snarling and snapping at the horse as he tried to get his teeth on Whip. Abruptly the horse quieted. Heck whined from his post on Whip's rear, and shot out a red tongue and lapped the horse's muzzle. The horse's ears came forward and the fiery heat seemed to melt from his eyes.

Dazedly, Jasper got to his feet and stood speechless with his men, the gun dangling in his hand. Heck lay down the length of Whip's back with his forepaws on Whip's rear. The dog whined softly and panted nervously as he watched the horse, his actions plainly protective of Whip, but not unfriendly toward the horse unless it threatened his master.

The dog allowed the horse to lower its head and smell Whip's leg, but nervously watched the horse's actions. The horse snorted once, then sniffed a second time. Then, as if he was licking salt, the big blue horse stuck his tongue out and tasted the cloth on the fallen rider's legs. He twirled his muzzle around and around on the cloth, closed his teeth on Whip's pants, took a small nip, then let go and licked the man again. The horse raised his head and gazed at the group of cowboys, then turned around and walked to the far side of the corral.

Whip moaned and Heck whined. The dog stepped off his master and went around to his face. By that time, Jasper had made it to Whip's side, and he knelt down and rolled him face up. One of the cowboys went to the horse trough and wet a neckerchief. Jasper put his ear close to Whip's nose and listened to his breathing.

Whip opened his eyes, blinked painfully into the sun, then shut his eyes again. The cowboy reached them with the dripping cloth, and Jasper cooled Whip's face. Almost immediately, Whip came back to grips with reality and sat up. He winced and grimaced, then set about testing the damage.

"Did I land on the fence or something?" he muttered, feeling his legs.

"No," Jasper said, "you got knocked out on his back, believe it or not."

"Never heard of it happening," Whip said, then grunted as he tried to stand up.

Jasper gave him a hand. Whip swayed a minute and winced again. He turned and looked across the corral at the blue roan, then started toward the horse.

"Hang on there, Whip," Jasper said. "You might be hurt inside. I don't think you'd better go another round with him right now. You almost met your Maker while you were out. If it hadn't been for Heck, that roan would have had you for lunch."

"What happened?"

"That outlaw came after you, but Heck jumped up on your carcass and held him at bay. I tell you, Whip, when a man's out like a dead man on a bucking horse, he's been hurt. I don't know for sure what happened, but you've been pert near jarred to death, and if you get back on that beast, I'll know your brain's just as jarred as the rest of you."

"Whip!" Ty cried from outside the corral. "It was too close. Listen to Jasper. You won't be lucky twice in the same day. Besides, Brownie's gonna be showing his face if my guess is right, and you'd better not be in anything but top shape. He said you were next, and he meant it."

"He said that?" Jasper asked, shooting a swift, hard look at Whip.

"What if he did?"

"I'd say you'd better start wearing that iron you got hanging on the peg, and I hope you've got a lot of ammunition! Come on down to the ranch and stay for a while. You and Ty are miles and miles from anyplace, and you're sitting ducks for Brownie," Jasper finished.

Whip pondered what Jasper had offered, and then looked at Ty standing outside the fence. "I'm no fool about Brownie. Jasper, you take Ty in for a while, though. He can't hold a gun in his hands, and I can't be beside him constantly. I stay here."

Whip turned away and went across the corral to the blue. He had no trouble getting hold of the reins. He felt bitter, knowing that the horse had come after him. He had never seen a horse run a man down but not attack him.

"Did he actually put his teeth into me?" he asked Jasper.

"Well, no, but, like I said, Heck stopped him."

"Did he pound me with a hoof?"

"No, he started to but . . . what are you fishing for, Whip?" Jasper asked.

"I don't believe this horse would kill a man out of meanness, and you haven't given me enough proof to believe he was gonna do it to me."

Whip stepped back beside the roan and uncinched the saddle. He pulled it off, then cleaned the hackamore off the horse's head with one skilled sweep of his hand.

"Believe what you want, Whip, but the dog saved your life, as far as I'm concerned. I'm glad to see you turn him loose," Jasper said. "What are your plans now?"

"I'd like to see Ty to the doctor just to have him checked out. Maybe the doc has something better for those knife cuts. Then I'd appreciate your doing what I ask. Take him in for a few weeks."

"I ain't leaving here!" Ty cried.

Whip turned back toward Jasper. "I'll get a couple of horses saddled."

Midafternoon found Whip and Ty, and Jasper and his cowboys halfway to Magpie Springs. As they rounded a bend in the river, they saw a group of riders lolling lazily under the shade of a cottonwood, one of the hundreds of barked giants that lined the river. About a half mile from the riders, Whip frowned as he stared into the distance.

"What is it, Whip?" Ty asked.

He ignored Ty and continued his vigilance. Like a flock of frightened sage hens, the relaxing riders leaped to their horses and fled, fording the river only minutes before Whip and his group rode up.

They found a few satchels, a woman's purse, and

some leather packets dumped out on the ground in the shade of the tree. A mail sack lay empty, its contents strewn about on the ground. Whip dismounted and the rest followed suit except for Ty, who couldn't help them pick up the mail even if he did manage to get off his horse.

"What do you make of this, Whip?" Jasper asked. "Do you think these villains robbed a pony-express rider?"

"No, looks more like a stage holdup. Look at the lady's purse." Whip studied Jasper's stricken face. "What is it?"

"My daughter is coming in on the evening stage!" Jasper ran to the knitted purse and opened it. Nothing was inside. He searched the ground and came up with a white handkerchief with *JAH* embroidered in a corner. "Whip, what were you looking at when we came riding up back there?" Jasper demanded.

"A horse. I didn't see a woman, if that's your next question," Whip said.

"But this is hers. What if she's been abducted? What if we're riding away from something we ought to be pursuing?"

"Well, Jasper, if there was a woman crossing that river, she's been acting like a man for so long I'd swap dukes with her and not feel bad about it."

"Let's ride," Jasper ordered, relieved at Whip's words.

Three hours later they rode into the town of Magpie Springs. The town was booming as far as business was concerned, and many new stores had opened up along its main street in the last five years. Two saloons fought for customers. Whip took Ty directly to the doctor while Jasper cantered off with his men toward the stage station at the other end of town.

It seemed only minutes later that Whip and Ty were unceremoniously ushered out the door of the doctor's office.

"Well," Whip growled, "you'd better not moan and groan to me about the scars on your face or the way your fist is throbbing."

"He didn't have no idea what to put on these cuts. All he did was shake his head and suck his teeth. If he had said 'my, my, my' one more time I'd have clamped his mouth shut with one of them shiny things on that tray!"

"He was trying to help you, you vile-tempered polecat," Whip said.

"Well, I just had to bust him in the teeth. He was getting so close to my face that I thought he was gonna kiss me. I had to bust him, Whip."

Whip helped Ty upon his horse, and then mounted his own. They let the horses drag along slowly, observing Magpie Springs as night fell. Pianos plunked in both drinking establishments, and a din rolled out into the broad street. Whip saw Jasper's mounts tied up in front of the sheriff's office. They rode up, and Whip dismounted and asked Ty if he wanted to come in, but Ty shook his head.

For some reason, Ty always avoided the sheriff of Magpie Springs.

As Whip entered the sheriff's office, the lawman was engaged in an argument with Jasper.

"I'll see we get another man in this office next year!" Jasper yelled.

"And he'll do no different than I'm doing. My job is in this town. If you want to run helter-skelter over the brush out there, go ahead. The stage is the responsibility of the territory. My suggestion is that you march down to the telegraph office and ask the U.S. marshal's office for help. Now get out, Hunt! I don't like being pushed!"

"Blast you, Reams!"

The sheriff walked to the door, nodded politely to Whip, then swung it open and turned back toward Jasper.

"Air ain't so stale out on the boardwalk, Hunt. Try it out."

Jasper puffed up like a toad, started to argue again, then stomped out into the night air. His men followed. Whip started to step out, but Sheriff Reams stopped him.

"How's your pardner?"

"He's gonna make it."

"Sorry to hear what happened. I've heard Ty's worth his salt. By the way, Whip, if the trouble is as bad as Hunt says it is out there, you'd better start wearing a gun."

"I reckon," Whip answered.

"Can you hit the broad side of a barn?"

"Possibly," Whip said.

"Well, practice. The only thing worse than a man without a gun in a pinch is a man that can't use one in a pinch. Buy some ammunition and learn to shoot. Don't tell Jasper, but I'm no fool about Brownie's activities or the danger of him."

"Neither am I."

"One of these days he's gonna come uncorked in this town, and I'm dreading it, because I know I can't stop him by myself. I guess I'm just playing for time, hoping somebody will get Brownie before it's forced on me to take care of something I already know I can't handle."

"Good night, Reams," Whip said, and turned to leave.

"One more thing, Whip. Can you tell me a little more about Jasper's rustled stock?"

"What happened?"

"Well, one of his men came in this afternoon and said somebody had herded off a bunch of steers. I guess some of Jasper's crew found where somebody had stopped long enough to brand and earmark the bunch before moving them out of the area."

Whip walked out into the darkness, and he studied the street a while before he went to his horse. Jasper had left, but Ty still sat on his horse, waiting for Whip.

"You're going home with Jasper," Whip said.

"Whip, I don't want—"

"I'd sure hate to plant a fist on your pretty scars, Ty," Whip said, mounting his horse.

"All right. Guess there ain't no use arguing with you. Jasper is down at the stage station. His boys said he's having trouble with his daughter."

"Let's go," Whip said.

At the station, Whip helped Ty dismount near the buggy that Jasper had rented from the livery, and then they entered the stage depot. No conversation was being exchanged, and they stepped right into a tense atmosphere.

The old rancher glanced at Whip, then gestured futilely toward the turned back of a young woman. She was fidgeting with something in her hands, then Whip saw her raise a handkerchief to her face, take a deep breath, and turn around. He was impressed. Jasper's daughter wasn't a beauty who knocked a man for a spin, but she had pleasing features that warmed a man's heart.

"Whip, this is my daughter, Jessica. Jessica, meet the best bronc rider in the country, Whip Cordeen."

Whip nodded at the girl, noting the shine in her hair in the dim lamplight, and the dimples that dodged in behind her smile as she acknowledged him. She appeared to be in her early twenties.

"Glad to meet you, Mr. Cordeen," she said.

"My name's Ty," Ty said, "and I ain't usually so ugly, but I had some bad luck, ma'am. I'm sure glad to meet you."

"Call me Jessica, please."

"I understand there's a problem, Jasper," Whip said.

"I reckon, and I sure don't want to be standing here butting heads with you, girl," Jasper said, seeming to speak to both Jessica and Whip at the same time. "But it's important that I return to the ranch immediately because my steers have been rustled. I don't have time to take you out where we found the items from the stage holdup."

Whip saw an opportunity, and he was quick to act on it. It was clear that Jessica had affected every one of Jasper's cowboys the same as she had affected him. This was a girl whom any one of them would court if she'd just give him the chance.

"I'm not in a hurry to be anywhere, Jasper," Whip said casually. "Maybe Miss Hunt would allow me to drive her out where we found the stuff from the stage. I could drive her on down to the ranch for you, and it would solve the whole problem."

Ty squinted a shrewd eye on Whip. Jasper's cowboys immediately informed Jasper that they could perform this task also. Jasper waved his hands and ordered everybody to quiet down. He turned to his daughter.

"Jessica, would it be all right if Whip drove you, so I can go on out to the ranch? I might be gone when you get there, but Mrs. Valez will be around. She's my housekeeper and cook. You wouldn't be alone, and Ty is gonna be staying with us for a while."

"Yes, I'd like that. I'm sorry for the trouble, but

I must look through the things you found," she said.

Jasper's cowboys moaned and looked a little forlorn. Then Jasper put his hands on her shoulders and looked into her eyes.

"I'm sorry, Jessica, I had so much looked forward to this meeting, but things seem to be working against me."

"It's all right, Father. I'll be fine, and we can catch up on our chatting later. Don't worry, I understand."

Jasper gave her a hearty hug. Whip felt triumphant when he saw Jasper's cowboys roll their eyes and look as if they'd swap everything they owned to trade places with him.

As the men filed out of the depot, Whip got some looks that hinged on aggression, except that none of the crew wanted to risk running into one of Whip's fists because of a look dropped now that he might remember later.

Suddenly the stage station became quiet. Whip wasn't a man easily rattled by a pretty lady, but this situation had suddenly become awkward. He flipped through some flattering remarks he had used in the past, but discarded them immediately. He had changed through the years. He felt calm as he decided to just be himself.

"I'll load your bags on the buggy. Where are they?" he asked.

"The large ones are over there." She pointed to

them. "But the smaller ones were taken by the bandits."

Whip loaded the baggage onto the buggy and tied it down. Then he led his horse over to behind the buggy and tied it. Returning to the station for Jessica, he realized that she didn't have a coat on and the night would turn chilly soon.

"Do you have a coat?" he asked.

"Yes, but it's in one of the trunks you took out and put in the buggy."

He had secured the trunks in the back of the buggy, and he had no intention of untying them again. He went to the wall where several coats hung. Nobody was using them at the moment, so he quickly appropriated one and handed it to her. She took it from him, but held it away from her.

"Whose is this?" she asked.

"I have no idea."

"Well, I don't intend to wear it."

"Wear it," Whip said firmly.

She let go of the coat and it fell to the floor. Whip glared at it, then at her. She glared at him just as sternly.

"Mr. Cordeen! You cannot order me around!"

"Yes, ma'am, I can. You're in my care until you're safely home. You're not going to get sick. You're going to wear the coat."

"Mr. Cordeen, you will please leave me to take care of myself. I will not be bullied by you, sir!"

Whip hadn't planned on an argument, and he was perplexed for a moment. He wanted peace, but she had drawn a battle line, and he wasn't the kind of man to give in to her, no matter how much he'd like to stay on friendly terms.

"Miss Hunt," he said, "I'll not leave you, and I advise you that it would be much more ladylike for you to walk to the buggy, but if you insist that I carry you. . . ."

"Don't you dare!"

"Miss Hunt, daring me wasn't the thing to do."

Whip reached for her, but she dodged him and tried to run out the doorway. He caught her around the waist, turned her in his hands, lifted her up over his shoulder like a sack of potatoes, and then carried her out on the boardwalk and down the steps to the buggy. She pounded his back with her fists.

"Put me down! How dare you! Put me down!"

A voice cut through the night air. "What you got there, Whip?" Sheriff Reams asked.

Whip turned with Jessica still over his shoulder. He felt stupid and embarrassed by this turn of events.

"Jasper's daughter. I'm escorting her home."

"Can't she walk?"

"She wouldn't."

"Well, be careful when you put her down."

Reams shot a crooked grin at Whip, aware of his embarrassment, and then he strolled on down the walk.

"Officer!" Jessica wailed. "Officer, he's a beast! A villain!"

"I doubt it," the lawman replied.

"Aren't you going to help me?" she cried after his fading boot steps.

"Nope. You ain't in trouble."

Whip put her down on the buggy seat and stepped back. He wasn't expecting what happened next. Jessica slapped him across the face, not once but three times, so quickly that it was over before it really got started. Whip felt like slapping her back, but he knew that a man never did that to a lady. He looked her directly in the face without speaking. She fidgeted under his savage eyes, then suddenly lifted a hand to slap him again. Whip caught her arm in midswing.

"I don't know what kind of men you're used to dealing with, Miss Hunt," he said icily, "but out here you don't slap a man, same as you don't dare him."

Whip felt her relax her arm, and he released his grip. He stepped up the rung, sat down beside her, and clucked to the horse, and they quickly left the town of Magpie Springs.

Whip drove in silence for a couple of miles, then suddenly pulled the buggy to a stop and turned toward Jessica.

"Miss Hunt, it seems you won that round. I forgot the coat. Show me which trunk you packed your coat in."

CHAPTER FOUR

UNDER the rustler moon, its slice of frost barely glinting the leaves and brush in silver light, Whip and Jessica rode silently. The clip-clop of the trotting buggy horse and the occasional creaking and squeaking of the buggy dominated surrounding noises.

Jessica pulled her coat more snugly around her shoulders, not so much from the cold but as a protection from the cool silence of her escort. The buggy sped along next to a silvery river that sparkled in the moonlight like millions of diamonds rolling along in the darkness. Captivated by its beauty, she turned to say something to Whip about it, and then withdrew into herself again. It was a long while later that she finally spoke:

"Mr. Cordeen, what is a girl supposed to do out in this country when a man deals rashly with her? I certainly am not strong enough to fight with a man like you. Slapping you was the only way I knew of to tell you to keep your hands to yourself.

I am not a sack of grain, and I resent being treated like one."

Whip didn't answer. He continued to drive the buggy horse, his eyes darting around occasionally to assure the safety of their travel.

"If you expect me to accept the idea that the women in the West allow themselves to be manhandled, I don't believe it," she said.

"I did what I thought was best to ensure your comfort," Whip told her. "That wasn't good enough for you, for some reason. I insisted because it was right. You dared me to defy you, Miss Hunt. *You* slung out the challenge. *I* didn't start the dang uproar."

"Well, Mr. Cordeen, are you a man that no one can defy?" she asked, sounding like it was something rather unacceptable in him.

"Usually," Whip said.

Moments later he pulled the buggy to a halt. He stepped down and tied the horse, then went to help her down from the buggy. She drew back from his hand.

"Is this the place?"

"Yes, ma'am."

"I will get down by myself."

"Miss Hunt, we're about to get into it again. I consider you a lady in spite of my earlier behavior, which you call rash, even though you're the one that asked for it. A man helps a lady down when he's in her presence, and, by gum, I'm not going to allow you to belittle my right to be a gentleman."

"Mr. Cordeen, I will not tolerate such behavior."

"Miss Hunt, take my hand and step down—now!"

Something leaped inside her, and it felt like a fear of angering this particular man at the moment. Jessica extended her hand, which he took gently. Then he steadied her as she stepped off the buggy. Suddenly she felt better, almost at peace with the man.

"Thank you, Mr. Cordeen," she said.

"My pleasure, Miss Hunt," Whip answered.

He let go of her hand and walked under the spreading boughs of the cottonwood. Little could be seen of the strewn articles in the darkness.

"There's a wax lamp on the buggy post. I'll get it," Whip said.

He struck a light to the wick, then sheltered the flame with his open palm. Jessica bent down and examined several articles of clothing. Suddenly she became excited and sat down on her heels, feeling a blouse that had many pockets. She opened the pockets one by one, then came upon an open pocket flap. There was nothing inside.

"Oh, no!" she moaned.

"What was it?" Whip asked.

"An engraved gold pocket watch that Mother toiled to pay for. It had my picture in the locket lid. We worked on this, Mother and I, so we could give it to Father for his birthday. Oh, Whip! It was so special."

She wasn't aware that she had used his first

name, but he was. He gave her a few minutes with her thoughts before he spoke.

"Gather up your things and we'll get on our way. Miss Hunt, I suggest you don't tell Jasper about the watch. It may be recovered if the thieves get caught in the near future. Is there anything special about the case that would help identify it?"

"Yes," she said. "The outside back has Father's name inscribed on it. Inside, behind my picture, it says 'For Father, Love Jessica.' "

"Well, we better get going," Whip said.

She nodded and began to gather up clothes. Whip left the wax lamp near her and stepped out into the darkness, checking the immediate area for danger. He found nothing and turned back, but froze in his tracks when he heard an animal crossing the river. The sound was going away, so he figured it to be a wild animal escaping the lantern light. He returned to Jessica.

"Where did you go?" she asked. "I got quite a fright, Mr. Cordeen. I thought I heard something, and when I looked up, there was a man sitting on a magnificent black horse. He laughed and then said something strange. He said, 'Tell Whip I said hi.' Then he turned his horse down that bank near the river and disappeared. If he wanted to talk to you, why didn't he just wait a minute?"

Whip stared at her, feeling a cold sweat on his brow. And then an anger almost beyond control.

"Get in the buggy," he said.

"Mr. Cordeen, will you stop ordering me around!"

"Get in the buggy," he snapped, then lost his patience and grabbed her by the wrist and pulled her along beside him at a rapid pace. Having helped her up to the seat, he returned to the lamp, picked up the few bundles she had put together, and blew out the light. He put away the lamp, placed her things in the back, then rummaged in his saddlebags and pulled out his gun belt. He strapped on the .45, and knew from the feel that it hung where he wanted it. He bent and tied the latigo, walked around to the other side of the buggy, and then stepped up and sat down. She saw the gun immediately.

"What's wrong?" she asked.

"The man you saw is named Brownie. If you ever see that black horse again, hide, Jessica. Your life might depend on it. Brownie is a killer. Remember Ty's face?"

"What happened?"

"Brownie caught him fishing, and beat him to a pulp and then carved up his face with a knife. Something bad is in the wind, and it's unfortunate you've come to this country at this time. I strongly suggest you return home."

"I can't, Whip. This is my home now. Mother died two weeks before I left. This was supposed to be a visit, but now it has to be forever. There's nothing back there for me. Oh, Whip! How can I tell Father?" She buried her face in her hands.

Whip reached out and put a comforting arm around her shoulders. "I got a hunch you'll find a way, and it'll be the right way, Jessica. Let's get you home."

Whip drove on through the night, seldom answering her questions, but when he did, it was his old nature, brief and to the point. He'd talked more in the last week than he had in ten years. Just before dawn, he drove the buggy into the courtyard at Jasper Hunt's ranch.

Ty got to his feet from a chair up on the spacious rambling porch and came forward to meet them, halting just at the top of the steps. He was babying his broken hands more than before. Whip got out and tied the buggy horse, but when he turned to help Jessica, he saw her standing, and lifting her long dress in order to see the step beneath her feet on the side of the buggy. She felt cautiously with her small boot.

"Miss Hunt," Whip said warningly.

She halted and turned her head. The reproachful look in his eyes was something she'd have to reckon with if she got down by herself. He would retaliate in some way, but Jessica had no intention of letting him intimidate her, and she was positive that, at the moment, in front of her father's house, he wouldn't dare do a thing. She alighted quickly, but before she could step away from the buggy, Whip was right beside her.

He clasped his hands around her waist and lifted her like a sack of feathers and placed her back up on the buggy. Jessica gasped and frowned, then immediately stepped down by herself, avoiding Whip's attempt to take her hand. He got hold of her again, and this time wasn't so gentle putting her back up.

"Stop it, Mr. Cordeen, or I shall call for my father!" she said defiantly.

"Take my hand, Miss Hunt," Whip said.

Jessica dodged his extended arm and started down off the buggy again. He grabbed her around the waist a third time, before she reached the ground, and he promptly stood her back up on the buggy.

"Mr. Cordeen!" she snapped, her blue eyes filled with fight.

She started down again and he put her back. Suddenly she spun around and leaped off the other side of the rig. She had taken a few strides before Whip rushed around to her side. As he caught her, she twisted and swung an open palm at him. He grabbed her wrist, hesitated for a minute, then threw her over his shoulder and toted her around the back of the buggy to the side where he had been trying to help her down. Jessica kicked and beat on his back with her fists. Once she twisted enough to get a handful of his hair, but Whip merely reached up with his free hand and pried her fingers open. He put her down in the buggy so hard that she thought her feet were going to go through the floor. Her head popped soundly enough to dislodge a large hairpin, and shimmering cascades of long blond hair tumbled down around her shoulders.

Jessica looked around desperately for help, but the only onlookers were Ty and a gracious-looking woman whom she knew must be Mrs. Valez.

"Get Father!" she called to the woman.

"He has gone," the woman said, smiling. "Miss Hunt, you would do well to allow Whip to help you down."

Jessica wilted inside. First the sheriff and now her father's housekeeper refused to come to her aid. They seemed to think that anything Whip did was perfectly all right.

"Mr. Cordeen," she said, "I don't want your help!"

"That's nothing you can control. You have it and you'll accept it," Whip said.

Jessica looked up at the sky, sighed, and held out her hand. Whip took it gently and helped her down. Once on the ground, Jessica hesitated to attempt dodging around him. She looked up into his gray eyes.

Whip was enchanted. The morning sun bounced gilded rays off the soft waves that fell down over her shoulders. Her lovely features seemed to be framed in soft gold. She was too pretty to seem real. He took a step back, but didn't let go of her hand. He tugged gently and she came forward, so he released her hand and slipped his arm under her elbow. They walked to the porch without speaking.

"Good day, Miss Hunt," Whip said softly, then

let go of her and touched his hat brim. "Ty, come down here and chat with me a minute."

Ty came down the steps, bashfully nodded at Jessica, but went around her as she climbed the steps. He followed Whip to the back of the buggy.

"For heaven's sake, Whip, that was uncouth and uncalled for. Jasper is gonna be mad as all get-out when he finds out you manhandled his daughter. What's the matter with you?"

"I didn't do any damage."

"Well, you sure didn't handle her the way a man ought to handle a lady like that."

"Don't lose any sleep over it, Ty," Whip said angrily.

"What's eating you?"

"Brownie."

"I figured something had taken place, because you're wearing that gun again. What happened?"

"He's here to stay and he's gonna push. Something's about to pop. Did Jasper stop at the telegraph office before he left town last night?"

"Yes."

"Well, I've got to get back to the spread fast," Whip said.

"Why?"

"Because Brownie knows I'm a long way from home. Jasper will have to return this horse and buggy. What happened to your hands again, Ty?"

"Oh, one of Jasper's boys let his mouth get out of hand concerning a scarred-up man's chances of winning a wife. I punched him with my left."

"And the doc with your other, right?"

"Yeah, but both them whacks was worth the discomfort."

Whip mounted, and after a look back at Jessica, he turned his horse and rode for home. He breathed a sigh of relief when he crossed the valley and saw his cabin on the hill and the hobbled horses grazing in the nearby countryside.

Heck came running to meet him. Cat chanced coming about a third of the way, then fairly flew over the ground toward the cabin as Heck became aware of his presence and whipped back through the tall grass in pursuit. Whip saw the blue roan watching him over the corral fence.

"I like you, Bandit Blue," he muttered.

Quite accidentally, Whip had so named the horse, and the name would stick. He unsaddled at the shed and turned his horse loose. Ambling over to the corral, he watched the roan go over to the far side. The horse's ears moved incessantly, but its eyes remained soft.

"I don't believe you tried to kill me," Whip whispered, then turned and went to the cabin for some chow.

The day was ending when he emerged from the cabin. He hadn't had any sleep for a long while. This was no time to work horses, but he needed to pen the finished horses so he could ride them once more tomorrow before he delivered them to the Cowan ranch, eighty miles to the southeast. Two old reliable horses, used for snubbing, stood switching flies near the roan's corral. Whip saddled one and headed into the pasture with Heck to bring in the horses.

Less than an hour later, the large corral was full of horses previously ruined but with a new outlook on life. Heck was in his element, doing most of the herding and penning himself, and clearly disappointed when the work was over. Whip turned his horse loose just as the sun started to sink beyond a far ridge. He strolled over to the roan's pen and gazed at the horse. Heck slid under the bottom pole, meandered over, and lay down at the animal's feet. Whip watched for a minute, then gave in to a desire to enter the corral.

He had no trouble getting close without spooking the roan. He moved in sideways to the horse, then knelt down beside the dog, a dangerous action because he had put himself totally at the horse's mercy. Whip had to know. He just couldn't believe the horse was a killer, but he also knew that this was all foolishness on his part. If the horse was bad, he'd never live to remember it.

Gently he petted Heck on the head, careful not to make any swift motions that would spook the horse standing over him. Only a few minutes had passed when he felt the horse's muzzle tapping at his hat. Suddenly the horse snatched the hat in its teeth, jerked it off his head, and spit it out. Whip continued to pet the dog.

A moment later he felt the horse's muzzle twirling around and around in his hair. The horse licked his head, dropped its silky wet tongue down onto his forehead, then worked the pink feeler around to one of Whip's ears. That seemed to be the extent of his investigation of the broncobuster. Bandit Blue went back to switching flies, proving to Whip that his meanness was man-made.

Whip shifted his weight, sat down Indian style in the corral dust, and pulled Heck into his lap. He scratched the dog's ears. A contented smile stayed on Whip's lips, and there was a light in his eyes that could be seen only in the eyes of a man who loved horses.

It was late when Whip finally stirred himself. Bandit Blue shied slightly and backed off a couple of feet as Whip stood up. He picked up his hat, spoke to the dog, and they went to the cabin. A lantern burned briefly inside; then the cabin went dark.

Whip was usually up before daybreak, but the early-morning sun was the first thing to greet the cabin door the next morning. Whip had overslept.

When he first opened his eyes, he had to stifle a yelp, then let his breath whistle through his teeth. He groaned and tried to turn his head, but his neck felt like a boulder twice the size of his head. The pain in his back went clear to his toes. He tried to bend his legs and crawl out of bed, but his knees refused, reminding him of the sensation he felt in his neck. He threw back the blanket and gazed at his knees, unable to understand what had happened to him.

Both joints looked like they were full of something just under the skin. He felt them, gently at first, then squeezed hard with his fingers. The skin dented and stayed that way.

He lay back and stared up into the rafters overhead. Apparently what Jasper had said about his being knocked out on the horse long before he got dumped was true. He had been hurt but he didn't know it. He pondered a few minutes, trying to figure out what to do. He had work to get done, and he forced himself to his feet, hissing out breath as he stiffly got dressed. He hurt like he'd been stomped under a bull, but all he'd done was to stay in the saddle. He thought that fact over a bit, and came to the conclusion that any man who rode Bandit Blue to a standstill would probably never live out the day. He headed for the corrals without breakfast.

Before noon rolled around, Whip had ridden nine head to a good lather without abusing a single one. Most of his aching stiffness had worked itself out as he rode, and after eating a good-sized lunch, he returned to the corral, and by midafternoon had seventeen head ridden down and ready for the trip to their new home.

He felt a great pride in what he and Ty had accomplished with the reconditioned outlaw horses. Not one had shown Whip anything but an honest, big-hearted desire to work. An outlaw horse was usually one with more intelligence and more heart than the average animal. Therefore, when a man made a mistake with it, it made a bigger impression on the horse's mind than it did on the mind of a normal horse. Then to top it off, the outlaw horse probably had more strength and size to back up its retaliation to human ignorance and cruelty.

Heck trotted beside Whip as he strolled over to Bandit Blue's pen. Any time there was spare time, Whip was drawn to the corral. He knew he'd be a fool to try to ride the horse in his present condition, and, again, he might be able to stay aboard, though doing so might get him killed. Whip continued to study the blue, wondering how the horse's own bones could take such a devastating impact. It would be nice if he could get on him in a deep snowdrift. That was it! Whip suddenly straightened up excitedly. The river, that was the answer!

He quickly saddled an old, reliable snubbing horse and then put his breaking saddle on Bandit Blue. Heck whined as he watched Whip nervously.

"Don't fret, Heck. I got a brainstorm that's gonna take the jolt out of this earthquake."

Whip soon had the snubbing horse into Bandit Blue's pen, and he dallied the long rope of the hackamore around the saddle horn, leaving the looped rein over the horse's neck. Out of the corral the little procession went, Whip mounted in front, Bandit Blue, then Heck bringing up the rear.

It took about a half hour to reach the river in the valley below, and once there, Whip traveled along the banks looking for a place with sandbars on both sides and deep water between. A quarter mile down the waterway, he found just such a place. First he took off his gun belt and hung it over a dead cottonwood limb. Then he spurred the balking snub horse out into the water, dragging Bandit Blue into the swirling current. The roan fought for only seconds, then followed into the deepening pool.

Whip maneuvered the snubbing horse alongside the roan, keeping both horses facing the same way. He kicked out of his stirrups, slid into the saddle on the roan's back, then let go of his snubbing horse. He took a deep seat and snugged down his hat.

The roan waited for Whip to turn him, something every man who'd ever attempted to sit his back had done first. To be left just standing confused the blue immensely. His ears continued flicking forward and back as he tried to understand his rider.

Suddenly Whip felt the horse's back heave upward, but the motion was also forward. The roan thrust so powerfully with its hind quarters that it entirely cleared the surface of the river. The roan's head dropped between its front legs because Whip gave him full rein. When the roan began its downward descent, instinct told it that something was wrong. The skillful rider grinned when he felt only the impact of the gigantic blue horse doing a super big belly flop when they splashed back into the river.

Bandit Blue's head went beneath the surface and

he soundly thumped his nose on a hermit boulder on the river bottom. He squealed and snorted water as his head flung upward, shaking the river out of his ears. Unable to handle the shock of the turn of events, the big roan exploded in fury. He leaped upward again, but his return to earth was wet and what little jar there was proved ineffective. He buried his head beneath the surface twice more as he plummeted down in an attempted piledrive. Then, suddenly, there was no bottom under his hooves. Whip and Bandit Blue both went beneath the surface. Then the powerful horse broke water and propelled himself and his rider smoothly across the pool, swimming easily.

Whip was grinning. His eyes twinkled and a low laugh voiced itself.

"Outthought you, horse, that's what I did!" Whip said in loud delight, slapping the horse's neck.

Twenty feet from the far shore, the roan touched bottom and tried another savage buck, but the bottom sank away and he had to swim or drown. The horse had too much intelligence to drown himself. Whip turned the horse downstream, staying in water saddle-horn deep, and rode it up and down the sandy bottom of the river. As the sun began to slip behind the hill, he finally allowed the worn-out horse to stop in knee-deep water.

Being forced through the water for a long time had taken the horse's mind off trying to throw its rider. The horse's ears were relaxed, sometimes listening to the rider, sometimes pricking toward the bank where Heck lay, waiting patiently for Whip to head home.

Now came the part that Whip dreaded. The snubbing horse had headed home on its own, and he hated walking in wet boots more than anything else he could think of at the moment. What would Bandit Blue do once he got out of the water? The only way to find out was to ride the horse onto the sandbar.

Whip nudged the horse forward, not totally sure he wanted to reach solid ground. The horse had barely lifted his hind feet out of the river when Whip felt him roll his back under the saddle. The horse snorted and tried to pull the rein out of Whip's hands by bobbing its head. Whip told himself he was about to bump his head on a cloud.

Before Bandit Blue's bunched up muscles thrust him heavenward, Heck leaped to his feet, barked, and disappeared behind the bank. The horse suddenly threw up his head, totally uninterested in the rider on his back. He blasted a shrill whistle in the direction Heck had gone and trembled clear to the tip of his tail hairs. Whip felt it coming, but couldn't stop it before it happened.

Bandit Blue swept upward like a Pegasus, but his momentum was forward more than up. He came back to earth and pounded down on the sandbar in a dead run, swerved, and leaped the six-foot bank, half stumbling at the top. Then he leaped away, his ears pricked forward and searching for

Heck. Whip saw the dog the same time Bandit Blue did. Cat had made the mistake of coming too far, and was halfway down the hillside when he realized his mistake and saw Heck converging on him like a boulder in an avalanche. Cat streaked for home, Heck streaked for Cat, and Bandit Blue just streaked.

Whip started to jerk the horse's head sideways, but at the speed it was traveling, he realized that one jerk would turn the horse upside down and probably kill them both. Whip settled down into the saddle, not pleased with the ride, but wise enough to help the blue stay on his feet over the rough terrain instead of fighting him.

It took only a few hundred feet for Whip to realize that he was astride the fastest horse he'd ever been on in his life. Bandit Blue was bred to run, and that he did.

It had taken a half hour to get to the river, but Whip doubted it took more than a few minutes to reach the scrub cedar below the cabin. Cat made it to a tree and zipped up to the top limbs with a bitten tail. Heck had almost had Cat for an afternoon snack. The dog was running around and around the cedar when the roan put on the brakes and slid to a stop, so abruptly that Whip was almost unseated.

The horse heaved for wind, its breath whistling in and out as it walked over to Heck and put its nose on the dog. Heck moved away, but Bandit Blue continued to stand with his head down, gasping for air. Whip stepped off. He rubbed a fond hand across the horse's white-lathered neck.

"You almost hurt yourself. Come on, let's walk you out a little."

Fifteen minutes later, the roan had stopped his heavy breathing and was walking docilely beside Whip, occasionally bumping his lowered head into Whip's leg. Between the work in the water and the three-mile run, Bandit Blue was played out. His body had been abused, but that abuse had been brought on by things that Whip could not control.

Heck lay in the shade of the tree and whined at Cat. The cat snarled and hissed back at Heck, looking constantly upward for a higher limb, but he was clear in the top of the cedar.

Whip looked up the hill, then gathered the reins and stepped next to the stirrup. He put one hand on the blue's neck and the other on the saddle horn as he mounted. The horse raised its head slightly at the feel of the man's weight in the saddle, but paid no more mind than to flick his ears back and turn his head to put a large, soft eye on Whip where he perched on his back. The horse blew out a deep breath, and Whip felt an excitement that almost brought tears to his eyes. Bandit Blue wasn't going to buck. He had accepted Whip's presence.

Whip rode the blue to the shed with Heck trotting at its heels. He unsaddled and brushed down the animal in the dusk of the evening. He wasn't normally a man to pamper a horse, but Bandit Blue got a liniment rubdown, a pan of oats, and a lot of kindly scratching before he was led to his pen and turned loose. The big roan walked to the water trough, drank, and then to top off Whip's day, it walked over to him and stood quietly. The cowboy gave him a firm rub on the neck. He considered himself the happiest bronc stomper in the Colorado Territory.

CHAPTER FIVE

AFTER supper Whip lit the fireplace and babied the fire into a hearty blaze. He put out the lamp, then sat back in his chair and let his thoughts get lost in the flames, reminiscing pleasantly over his ride on Bandit Blue that afternoon.

He didn't know how long he had daydreamed when Heck suddenly growled and got to his feet. The dog tilted his head and listened, rolling his eyes back and forth at nothing. He growled louder.

Whip got to his feet and went to the peg on the wall for his gun belt. It wasn't there. He was confused for a minute, then remembered where he had left it. Because of Bandit Blue's wild dash up the mountain and Whip's joy in the way things had turned out, he had never again thought about his .45, now hanging on a dead branch down by the river.

He took the carbine down from its rest. Since he had blown out the lamp earlier and let the flames of the fire do for light, he couldn't help the fact that he would be a silhouette for a moment when he stepped through the door. Whip ordered Heck to heel and opened the door. He closed it as soon as he got through it, then stood still while his eyes got accustomed to the dark. It wasn't totally dark, because a rustler's moon still hung in the sky, but its light was dim. Whip saw the horses in the corral mill about nervously, occasionally stopping to look out toward the valley.

He stepped off the porch, holding the carbine in a relaxed but ready grip. Heck looked out across the flat to where the mountain dropped in its descent to the valley, and he growled again. There was something going on. Whip cursed himself for his carelessness with the .45. If he had to ride, he'd prefer to have his six-gun on his hip and the carbine in a scabbard. Not having one or the other would be a drawback. The horses slowly settled down out in the big corral, but Bandit Blue continued to look out toward the valley. Heck suddenly lay down at Whip's feet with his nose on his paws. After several more minutes, Whip felt that the immediate danger, whatever it was, had passed. He called Heck to heel and stepped back inside.

Something had happened down in the valley. Whip spent a few minutes considering the location of his .45, then decided to go get it. He didn't want to be caught out in the open, pinned down in the dark with no ammunition, so he stuffed a box of carbine shells into his shirt. Then, realizing the possibility of getting cut off from his ammunition if there were trouble, he grabbed up a box of .45 shells for his revolver.

He called Heck again and walked back out the door. He had barely started for the corral when he heard Heck growl loudly and saw him look toward the cedars just over the brow of the hill. Changing his plans about saddling up a horse, Whip sneaked around the corrals to the scrubby brush of the cedars. Where Heck had looked was quite a walking distance from where he was at the moment. Whip again thought about saddling a horse, decided against it, and began stalking he knew not what in the pale dimness.

Heck growled off and on while they advanced. The minutes ticked by. As the time increased into an hour or more, Whip found himself on the edge of the cedars. Heck hadn't growled for a long while. Whip watched for many minutes; then, cautiously, checking every shadow, he started back over the brow of the mountain toward his cabin.

Suddenly, from between two trees, he saw a golden glow high on the mountain. Whip started, then began to run up the hill. Within minutes, still a quarter mile from the cabin, he could see flames licking above the tops of the cedars. He knew his cabin was going up in smoke, and he hurried as well as a man used to riding a horse almost every day of his life could hurry.

Three hundred yards from the cabin, the whole scene came into view. Riders were hazing his horses from the corrals, while a half dozen more left the roaring inferno of the cabin and mounted their horses. Whip threw the carbine to his shoulder, thought about the foolishness of giving away his position, and slowly lowered the gun. He quietly edged his way through the sparse cedars, sickly watching his home burn to the ground. Rushing now wouldn't save a thing. The riders were silhouetted against the flames as they drove his horses into the night. Suddenly the air was quiet except for the popping and crackling of the burning cabin. Like a specter, a dark horse and rider hesitated alone in the yard. Then the horse pranced for a minute and turned sideways in the bright light. Whip saw a string of reflections across the horse's chest and alongside its head. Silver conchas!

Abruptly the horse bolted and disappeared from Whip's sight into the pale night beneath the crescent moon. Numbly Whip walked back to what was left. Thankfulness also was a part of his thoughts at that moment. What if Ty had not gone to Jasper's? Only Heck's growl had gotten Whip out into the night, and even if Ty had been aware that Whip was out checking something, he would have stayed in the cabin and waited to see what turned up.

Whip stared at the open corral gate, then jumped, spooking when he saw something move out of the corner of his eye. There, head flung high, Bandit Blue stood penned, unable to follow the stolen herd.

Whip walked dazedly through the deep grass

and went up as close as he dared to the burning structure. The fire had peaked, and now it began to reduce itself to spots of burning among the charred remains. Ten minutes later, nothing but the fireplace stood where only hours ago he had dreamed in front of its warmth.

Whip walked over to the corral that restrained Bandit Blue. He pondered a few minutes, then went to the saddle shed. The door was open, but most of the gear was untouched. The outlaws didn't need gear. Whip wondered why they hadn't burned the saddle shed too.

He quickly found the hackamore and went to the corral. As he reached for the sliding bar, his eyes fell on a piece of paper wedged against the handle. He put down the hackamore and unfolded the paper. The light from the burning cabin was growing dim, and Whip had to walk a few dozen feet toward it in order to read the note.

Dear Whip,

Thanks for the reimbursement. I consider us even now for the death of two of my men who had a bit of trouble with that jewel you swindled off on me. I figure you'll need a saddle to ride that blue devil. For that reason, they are unharmed. He's all you've got left, so enjoy your ride. We are not even on another score. Hunt me. I dare you.

Your Old Friend

Whip folded the note and put it into his shirt pocket. He picked up the hackamore at the corral gate, went inside, brought Bandit Blue out through the gate, and led him to the saddle shed. He was silent as he pulled up the cinch on the saddle. Brownie was baiting him into pursuit. The reason escaped Whip, but the bait tonight had worked. He needed his .45, and the outlaw was right—he had no choice but to ride the renegade roan.

Whip watched the fire a minute, letting the blue get used to the saddle. He transferred the shells he had so luckily saved from his shirt to the saddlebags. He slid the carbine into the scabbard, then led the horse for a few minutes.

"Bandit Blue," he whispered as he gathered up the reins and placed the toe of his boot in the stirrup. "No man ever needed a horse more than I need you. Don't let me down, big roan."

Whip settled gently into the saddle. He felt a natural urge to shorten up his reins, but the loose rein did more to keep the roan on all fours than any other thing Whip could think of. He sweated out a few seconds, waiting for the horse to pile him in the darkness, and then whistled softly for his dog. As Heck walked up to the horse, he said, "Come along, Heck. I got a feeling this blue hide won't willingly go anywhere you don't go."

Whip took a deep breath and held it, sure that when he untracked the roan, the rodeo would begin. But, instead, the roan lowered his head and nuzzled the dog's coat. Whip tugged gently on the rope reins and Bandit Blue obeyed, lifting his head and stepping out in a brisk, long-reaching gait. The horse turned his head just enough to confirm Heck's presence at his heels, then put his efforts into covering ground.

At the river, there was plenty of light from the sky for Whip to locate his .45. He dismounted and picked up the gun belt, which he strapped around his hips. He gazed off up into the heavens. The moon seemed more like a rustler's leer after what had happened to him tonight. He pulled his gaze from the stars and let his hand rest on his gun butt as he let his eyes drift out across the river.

"I hate this iron, Bandit Blue. Why can't a man live without it if he wants?"

Whip stepped into the stirrup and mounted the horse. He didn't see Heck and whistled, but the dog was only a few feet away in a dark shadow.

Whip had no intention of trying to scurry off after the horse thieves at the moment. Since he couldn't prove who had written the note, trying to enlist the aid of Sheriff Reams was remote. But the note proved that Brownie wasn't planning to leave Colorado in the immediate future. Whip's first obligation was to let Ty know that he hadn't been burned to death in the cabin. Undoubtedly, he would be assumed dead if they didn't find him and saw the mess up on the hill. Whip thought about Cat and hoped the critter hadn't been under the cabin.

He turned the roan toward Jasper Hunt's ranch

and put the horse to a good, lanky lope. With Heck alongside, the horse didn't make the slightest indication that he'd like to run away again. As they covered country, Whip schooled the horse, teaching the animal to veer at leg pressure. He was a man who had to train a horse almost every minute he was on its back. He couldn't just ride along as a passenger or piece of baggage. Within a short while, however, he found that Bandit Blue already knew leg cues. He must have been trained before he was stolen, since none of the outlaws had been able to stay on him long enough to train him.

The sun was barely an hour in the sky when Whip rode Bandit Blue into Jasper's courtyard. A gathering of some kind was going on near the front porch. Every face turned toward the rider and his two companions as they loped into the yard. Whip pulled the roan down into a soft jog trot, then slowed him more and dismounted at a hitching rack in front of the porch.

Ty was so speechless that his mouth gaped open, and his eyes looked like they were going to pop out of his head. Jasper looked about the same. Whip heard a murmur from several of the men standing in a group near Jasper, and he saw the six cowboys who had seen Bandit Blue jar him cold right in the saddle.

"Down . . . stay," Whip ordered, snapping his fingers at Heck.

The dog walked under the big roan's belly and lay down, his tongue lolling out as he panted tiredly. Another murmur rumbled from the group of men, and then Jasper broke away from them and came up to Whip. As he offered his hand, Whip shook it and then looked up at Ty.

"We got burned out and cleaned out last night," Whip said.

With that information, Ty was able to pull his eyes off Bandit Blue and put them on Whip.

"What happened?" he asked, still dazed at Whip's mount.

"You heard me." Whip put a long look on his friend. "You're lucky. If you'd been there, you'd be a crisp."

"Must have been fast."

"And it was thorough. I'm going after him," Whip said.

Ty immediately threw a fit, all the way from begging Whip to cussing him soundly for his desire to pursue the outlaw. Only Ty could get away with chewing out Whip Cordeen.

"I know what you're doing, Ty, and it won't work. I'm going. Brownie made off with every horse we had on the place except Bandit Blue."

"Bandit Blue?" Ty said, looking puzzled. Then his eyes fell on the roan. "Well, it sure fits."

"Jasper, I need some grub. Can I fill my saddlebags here?" Whip asked.

"Of course, but wait for the marshal. I got the answer to my telegram. He's headed here as fast as he can put the miles behind him."

"Where's he coming from?"

"Creede," Jasper replied.

Whip tensed before his next question.

"What's his name?"

"John Wilhelm."

Whip stared at Jasper for a while, and then gazed off into the morning sky. Jasper looked at Ty, shrugged, and gestured futilely with his hands, unable to understand Whip's look, but reluctant to pry into the reason behind it. Whip swung his gaze back on Jasper.

"Don't yap about me, any of you," Whip said. He walked up the steps of the large porch and told Ty, "You have somebody keep an eye on our spread. If Bandit Blue comes back to the area, don't get worried, but if Heck and the roan both show up at the place, I'm either dead or in darn big trouble."

He turned away from Ty and glanced down at Jasper as he walked toward the ranch-house door.

"I'm in a hurry. All right if I help myself in the kitchen?"

"Sure, take whatever you need," Jasper said, eyeing the low position of the gun on Whip's thigh.

Whip had just stepped into the house when he ran into Jessica. She was coming out of a door as he strode toward the kitchen. They came together with a bump, but Whip clasped her quickly and kept her from falling.

"An accident, Miss Hunt," he said, releasing the grip he had on her shoulders.

"I hear you, but I'm not sure I believe it," she said.

Whip stepped around her and continued on into the kitchen. She followed him, then watched in amazement as he opened the cupboards and bins and took out food. He seemed to know where everything was stored. He reached down behind a wooden barrel and pulled out a sack that she didn't know was stashed there. She walked over to a chair and sat down, watching him thoughtfully.

"Was this your house once?" she asked.

"No," Whip answered, and continued to add items to the sack.

"How do you know where everything is stored?"

"I spent two years breaking horses for your dad. Things seldom change in a ranch's kitchen."

"Oh," she said. A moment later she spoke again: "I never knew there was so much food in a kitchen anywhere on earth before I came here."

"Why did you and your mother do without when Jasper's got more than any man needs?"

"Mother refused his money. She said that she loved him, but couldn't live out here, so she wouldn't take his money since she wasn't a fit wife. Father always believed that she would come here someday, but Mother had a dreadful fear of the West."

"It's fairly safe here at the ranch," Whip said.

"What are you doing?" she asked, suddenly putting the facts together when she saw him stuff in a small pan and coffee.

"Going for a ride."

"But you live only a little ways off. Why do you need all that food?"

"I have a job to do." Whip swung the bag to his shoulder. He gazed at Jessica, and a very strange look came into his eyes. She turned her head slightly and gave him an apprehensive glance.

"Why are you looking at me like that?" she asked.

Whip needed somebody to fight for other than himself, somebody to come back to when he had trips to make, somebody to think about out on the trail, and someone to hold just because he craved it. Jessica was a symbol of what he needed in his life. He walked over to her and looked down.

"I may not come back from this, Miss Hunt," he said, feeling like a rotten skunk for playing on her emotions to steal a kiss, but he went on with it.

"Is this dangerous, this ride that you're taking?"

"Deadly, ma'am," he said, then reached down and caused her to get to her feet by clasping a strong, gentle hand on her shoulder and lifting. "Wish me well, Jessica. I may never see you again."

"Oh, no," she whispered, her concern for his fatal job written all over her pretty face.

Whip felt a finger shaking at him from within his conscience, but he couldn't stop now. He bent down and kissed her lips, aware that the pity she felt for his ill fate and the surprise of what he did in that moment would render her into shock for the few seconds that he needed to steal a kiss. If he lingered too long, she would probably recover and slap his face.

Whip drew back and stepped around her, leaving her in mute shock, momentarily unable to regain her senses, but he was barely at the front door when he heard her running from the kitchen. He stepped out and shut the door.

Jessica saw him slip quickly outside with a sly backward glance. She pulled at the handle and tried to open the door. But it wouldn't open. She tugged hard, then suddenly realized that the power holding the door shut was Whip Cordeen.

"You thief!" she yelled, beating on the door with her fists. "You tricked me! You stole that! Let me out!"

Whip shot swift glances over his shoulder at Jasper Hunt, who now stood on the porch with Ty. He was in a pickle. If he let her out, she was going to retaliate and he'd have to take it in front of Jasper. He wanted more than anything else just to continue to hold the door shut until she calmed down.

"What's going on?" Jasper asked.

The old rancher frowned at Whip while he listened to his daughter's angry outbursts from inside. "Let her out, Whip," he said.

"Much as I'd like to do as you ask, I can't see the intelligence in that," Whip muttered.

"Well, I didn't ask you to see. Let her out. What in the world would make her think you stole something? Whip, doggone it, let her out so I can find out what's got her so upset."

Whip shot a worried look at Bandit Blue, knew he couldn't make a flying escape on a half-broken horse, then resigned himself to the fact that he was going to have to take what Jessica dished out. He had asked for it, but he couldn't stifle a grin as he remembered the warm softness of her lips on his, and how easily he'd attained her sympathy. He let go of the door.

Jessica leaped out, her face flushed and her blue eyes flashing like diamonds. She walked up to him and unhesitatingly slapped him so hard it almost brought tears to his eyes. She drilled her savage blues into his gray eyes for only a second, then slapped him again. Jasper lunged across the porch from behind Whip and grabbed her arms from behind.

"My gosh, girl! What are you doing?" Jasper gasped hoarsely. "You can't do that to Whip!"

"You sneaking cheat and thief," she yelled at Whip, trying to get loose from her father.

Jasper held her and tried to calm her. Suddenly Whip saw a tear brim on her eyelid, the first sign of the frustrating end to Jessica's indignation. She turned and tried to wrestle out of Jasper's clutches, but he held her.

"Jessica! Jessica! What's this all about?" Jasper asked.

"He—he kissed me!" she moaned, then ran into the house.

Whip turned about six shades of purple and he knew it. He put his free hand to his hat, pulled it down over his eyes, and quickly descended the porch steps. As quickly as he could without spooking Bandit Blue, he pulled the items out of the sack and shoved them into his saddlebags.

Jasper walked up close to him and watched Whip's progress. When Whip went around the horse to fill the other saddlebag, Jasper caught him by the arm, very carefully.

"Whip, I don't know what to do about this. I know you've done something rotten, but 'insult' is a strong word I don't want to use. What happened in there?"

Whip put a strong eye on Jasper. What he had done was between him and Jessica. There had been no insult intended, and he doubted that she felt that way. Probably mad and flabbergasted at his brashness, but not insulted. She had wanted to slap him for it, and he had let her. As Whip saw it, they were even.

"I kissed her, Jasper, but I didn't insult her. Didn't you ever steal a kiss?"

Jasper studied Whip a minute. Then a gentle grin crossed his features. He put a friendly hand to Whip's shoulder.

"The truth is, I never was able to pull it off, but I always wanted to. I don't think there's any harm done here, so congratulations, you fox. But I'll be watching you from now on."

Whip grinned, then continued on around the

roan and filled the other saddlebag. Ty came up and offered Whip his coat.

"I don't need it, and you're without one."

"Thanks," Whip said.

Ty and Whip studied each other for a bit. Whip knew that his death would probably be as bad on Ty as Ty's would on him.

"I'll be careful, Ty," Whip said, then went over to the horse's head and untied the hackamore rein.

A total silence descended on the courtyard as the cowboys watched Whip put his foot in the stirrup of the saddle that was cinched down on the most talked about terror on the range, its fame spreading like wildfire in recent days.

Whip mounted, hoping desperately that Bandit Blue would not embarrass him further and explode right in front of Jasper's men. No such thing came to be, and he heard exclamations of wonder as he nudged the roan out in an easy jog and called to his dog. His destination was about twenty miles east, where his stolen horses had left a wide path.

CHAPTER SIX

DEPUTY Marshal John Wilhelm sighed wearily as he stepped down from his horse in front of the sheriff's office in Magpie Springs and went inside. A bit later, he stepped out into the darkness with the strong feeling that the sheriff of Magpie Springs was scared stiff of Brownie and allowed the outlaw to run at will. Wilhelm had gotten directions to Jasper Hunt's ranch, and with that destination in mind, he headed his tired horse out of town.

Brownie was no stranger to John Wilhelm. He'd been after him for twelve years, and before that he was already a thorn in the side of the law and most settlers. Brownie had tried to move in on a section of Kansas about twelve years ago, but got his gang wiped out because of a mistake he'd made, and since that time, Wilhelm had gotten only gossip about his doings and whereabouts. Brownie wasn't the whole problem, though, because he was sure that his own office had been infiltrated by a couple of scoundrels. He had one of them pretty well pinned down, but the identity of the other eluded him, so this time he hadn't told anyone where he was going.

He needed sleep, but he was dedicated to the people he served as deputy marshal. He rode most of the night, camped on a ridge in view of but a couple of miles from the ranch, and slept out what was left of the darkness. The sun roused him, and he rode on to the ranch in the bright rays of the morning sun.

Jasper watched the rider approach, tense at first because of the darkness of the horse's color, but relaxed when he saw it wasn't Brownie. The man pulled his horse to a stop several yards from the hitching rack and sat his horse quietly.

Jessica was sitting beside her father on the porch. She glanced at the man and then at Jasper, but kept silent, waiting to see what was in the wind.

"Howdy, stranger," Jasper said quietly, scrutinizing the man.

"Are you Jasper Hunt?" Wilhelm asked.

"Yep. Who are you?"

"John Wilhelm. You sent for me."

"Got any proof of who you are?" Jasper asked.

Wilhelm pulled the left side of his coat aside and displayed a U.S. marshal's badge.

"Not good enough," Jasper said. "I want some identification."

"Come down here on my level and I'll show it to you," Wilhelm said, watching Jasper like a hawk.

Jasper descended the half dozen steps and stood by the hitch rack. Wilhelm dismounted and reached inside his coat. He handed a thin black leather fold to Jasper, but when the rancher reached for it, Wilhelm jerked it back.

"I want to see yours, Mr. Hunt," he said softly.

"I ain't got any," Jasper said indignantly.

"Well, then I'm not going to do any business with you."

Wilhelm stepped to the side of his horse as if to mount his chestnut. Jasper came from behind the rack but stopped when he realized he was chasing after the man.

"If you're Wilhelm, I don't want you riding off. I need help. Ain't my word good enough?"

"Isn't mine?" Wilhelm shot back coolly.

Jasper studied the lawman a minute, then extended his hand.

"Sorry about my rudeness. I don't trust Brownie as far as I can throw him, and there was always the chance you were an imposter. I trust my instincts, and they say you're true blue. Come up and have some coffee with Jessica and me."

Wilhelm took a chair against the wall, next to Jessica, and across the small table from Jasper. He waited as Jasper hollered at somebody inside the house. A minute later Mrs. Valez brought another cup and filled it with coffee. She set it in front of the lawman and smiled pleasantly as she said, "I'm so glad you're here. Whip has been gone for several days, and I fear he's taken on too much." Mrs.

Valez turned to go back inside, but Jasper asked her to bring a cup and join them. In a few minutes she returned with a cup of coffee and sat down beside Jasper.

"Who's Whip?" Wilhelm asked Jasper.

"About the toughest scrapper around. If you let him hit you, you'll regret it, but I'll bet you won't let yourself get in that situation again."

"Mean?" Wilhelm asked.

"Naw, there ain't a mean bone in his body. In fact, I'll bet he weeps every time he has to sell a horse. He's the best bronc stomper in the country."

"How is he with a gun?"

"Doesn't wear one . . . well, not usually. I never saw a gun on his hips until a couple of days ago after Brownie stole his horses. Whip went after him."

"Why didn't you go with the man?"

"I had some cattle rustled, and we caught the herd two days south of here. I rode back home immediately, but what cowboys weren't tied down here were bringing my cattle back. All the rustlers did was run brands. They didn't put any particular brand at all on their hides. Anyway, he wouldn't have let me go with him if I had asked. I told him you were coming, and all he said was, uh, well, nothing." Jasper had remembered that Whip had said not to yap about him.

"Sounds like you don't want me to know something," Wilhelm muttered, reaching for a cold pancake that topped a plate stacked with three or four. "Mind?" he asked.

"No, go ahead. Want some preserves or honey on it?"

"Nope, like them just like this. I'll tell you from experience, there's darn few men that can follow Brownie into a hideout without getting some lead between the shoulder blades."

"Brownie will never get Whip that way," a voice said from the doorway.

Wilhelm looked sideways and saw Ty standing near him. He looked the man up and down, then settled on his cut-up face.

Ty walked out on the porch and pulled up a chair with his wrist under the back board. His hands were still too tender to grab things. He sat down on the end next to Jasper and studied Wilhelm.

"Who are you?" Ty asked.

"Oh, 'scuse me," Jasper said. "John, meet Ty Holden, good cowboy but ailing a little after a run-in with Brownie. Ty, this is John—"

"Glad to meet you, Mr. Holden," Wilhelm said, breaking in on Jasper.

Ty nodded to the stranger and reached for Jasper's cup of coffee. Jasper skillfully whipped up the cup and held it out of Ty's reach, frowning like a thunderstorm.

"Keep your dukes off my coffee. Get your own," Jasper said.

"Aw, don't get your feathers ruffled. I couldn't get a hold on it, anyway." Ty looked at Wilhelm.

"What do you do, seeing as your dress says you're not a cowpuncher?"

"I'm the deputy marshal out of Creede."

Ty stared at him for a second, then scooted his chair back and got to his feet. He looked out across the courtyard for a bit, then spoke to Jasper.

"I plumb forgot something. See you later."

He started down off the stairs, but Wilhelm sprang to his feet and followed him. He put a hand on Ty's arm.

"I'm not after you, Holden. Sit down."

Ty looked down at the steps without turning at Wilhelm's words. The lawman's grip felt as strong as Whip's. He continued to stand like that until Wilhelm forced him to turn around.

"You know me?" Ty whispered, looking up at Wilhelm.

"I didn't recognize you at first, because of the cuts, but your name put your face to memory. Sit down."

Ty went back to his chair and sat down. He wouldn't look up for a few minutes, but when he did, he put his attention on Mrs. Valez.

"I'd like a cup of coffee, Tina," he said dejectedly.

A few tense minutes passed while they waited for Mrs. Valez. She returned with a two-handled cup that had been created for Ty by one of Jasper's cowboys. She set it down, then sat down and looked at the lawman.

"*Señor,* Ty is a good man," she said.

"I'm sure he is," Wilhelm said.

Ty looked up at the lawman with a puzzled expression on his face. John Wilhelm put a stern eye on Ty for a minute. Then his expression softened.

"I knew about a man who wasn't once, but then that was a long time ago. I often find that I forget seeing a man whose name doesn't keep coming to my attention."

Jasper gazed at Ty with an accusing eye. Ty had regrouped from his previous humbleness and had fallen back into his normal, testy self. Wilhelm had taken a load off Ty's mind that had worried him for a long time. He reacted to Jasper's expression, saying, "What are you staring at, you old buzzard?"

"What have you done?" Jasper demanded.

"Nothing you haven't."

"Let's get on with Brownie," Wilhelm told Jasper.

"Well, we found my steers just grazing on a large mesa without a rustler around when we caught up to them. It was stranger than a barking cat. We just kinda herded them together, and then the boys drove them home. What do you make of that?"

Wilhelm thought a moment, then allowed a chuckle to escape. "Another piece to a puzzle I've been laboring over for years. Every rustler I've ever dealt with has had a pattern of some kind. Not Brownie. I've got no answer for you. I think he's just trying to scramble my brains, and he's doing a darn good job of it."

"Why do you think Brownie's hanging around in this area?" Jasper asked. "There's only two large cattlemen, Cowan and me, and our cows are spread out over thousands of acres. It would take him weeks to round up a big enough herd to turn him a profit for his risk. Criminy, the herd he stole last week was only thirty-head strong. That's stupid, as I see it. Maybe that's what he finally figured out, and that's why he abandoned them."

"I doubt it, but I haven't got a better explanation at the moment." Wilhelm held up his empty cup and nodded at Mrs. Valez for a refill. He looked out across the rugged country for a few minutes.

"You know, you might have here just exactly what he's looking for. Thousands of acres and no law activity, judging from what I've seen of your sheriff in Magpie Springs. What Brownie may be trying to achieve is clearing out any men who will buck up against him, so he can run stolen cattle on this range without resistence. You see, that's where he erred before. He didn't clear the area of fighting men when he tried to move into a section of Kansas, and he found more than he could handle with my partner, Jim. Jim cracked down on the whole lot of them, but Brownie got Jim in the process. The gang was wiped out, but we lost Jim. Good man, darn good man." Wilhelm became lost in thought, but returned to the present when Mrs. Valez poured him more coffee. "Thank you," he said.

"So that's probably why he went after Whip's horses," Jasper observed thoughtfully.

"Why do you say that?"

"Well, if there was a man that could plant Brownie six feet under, it would be Whip," Jasper said.

"No, a man that isn't just plain greased lightning with a gun won't get Brownie. I know what you said about him being a fighting man, but Brownie is more than your man can handle." He put down his cup and stood up. "I'd like to get a few hours' sleep, then get a look around this country and try to locate my bandit."

"Easy to tell where he is," Ty said.

"It is? Well, enlighten me, cowboy."

"Whip went east and south. That means he's gonna cross Brownie's trail somewhere. Follow Whip's trail, and you'll find your man. But I wish you'd hurry, because I'm sure worried about my pardner."

Wilhelm turned to Jessica. "Mrs. Hunt, do you have a place I can lie down for a few hours?"

"Whoa, there, I ain't no cradle robber," Jasper protested. "Excuse me for not introducing you, but we got involved in the conversation too fast. John, this is my daughter, Jessica."

Wilhelm bowed his head, acknowledging his error. He removed his hat and said, "I would not have wasted idle words on these men had I known I could enjoy the morning more pleasurably in passing the time with you, Miss Hunt."

Jessica smiled and got to her feet. "Possibly, Mr. Wilhelm, but I doubt your words have been idle." As she led the way into the house, Wilhelm quickly caught up and walked in step with her.

"You have a pretty way with words, Mr. Wilhelm," she told him.

"Perhaps, Miss Hunt, but I'm a very married man, so ignore my pretty way with words," he said. "However, I would be delighted to have the privilege of your friendship."

"You have it, Mr. Wilhelm. When do you want to be awakened?"

"Early afternoon," he said. "Where do I put my horse to bed?"

"I'll have one of the cowboys do that." She indicated a room and Wilhelm stepped inside.

The sun passed high noon and began its travel across the last half of the sky. Jessica tapped lightly on Wilhelm's door, and a short time later, the man came yawning down the stairs. Jessica handed him his saddlebags and smiled.

"What's this?" he asked.

"I packed you cookies, dried beef, and some horehound. I hope you like it."

"I will, I guarantee it. Where's my horse?"

"Saddled and down at the barn."

"Come, walk me to my steed, fair lady," he said with a soft laugh and a bow. As they strolled toward the barn, he said, "I wish that Whip knew

Brownie a little better. I doubt he would have gone after him alone if he had known him."

"Oh, he knows Brownie real well. In fact, one night by the river, Brownie rode up beside me in the dark and said 'Tell Whip I said hi.' Then he just left without waiting for Whip, even though Whip had left me for only a minute. He was coming right back."

Wilhelm stopped in his tracks and stared at Jessica. He trembled slightly, then began walking again.

"Why did that bother you?" she asked.

"Brownie killed my partner years ago. Two nights before it happened, he walked up on me as I slept in my bedroll. Jim was out on watch. He must have shook me to wake me, and when I opened my eyes, I almost died. Brownie said those same words—only, he said, 'Tell Jim I said hi.' I've thought about it in the years since, and I think that's his way of saying, 'I'm gonna kill him.' Your friend Whip is in more serious danger than I suspected. I hope I'm in time."

Jessica knitted her brows and bit her lip. She recalled Whip's kissing her, and even though he had tricked her, she remembered him fondly because of it.

"I pray you are, Mr. Wilhelm," she whispered.

They had reached the barn, and as Wilhelm tied down the saddlebags, he thanked her for the food she had packed. Jessica gave him a brief description of the missing watch, in case John ran across it.

Then she watched him mount the chestnut and ride out of the barn with a wave of his hand.

Whip broke camp near a roaring river. He saddled Bandit Blue and mounted, studying the wide trail left by the horses on the far side of the valley. He had no intention of following near the trail. His pursuit had been at a snail's pace, moving only when he was totally sure of advancing safely. Patience was life when a man followed Brownie.

The water was too vicious for the dog to negotiate, so Whip called Heck up into the saddle with him, and then moved Bandit Blue out into the current. They splashed up the far bank and immediately Heck jumped down. Whip reined the roan toward the heavy timber. He knew where the horses had gone up the mountain, and he spent a long while making his way, in order to avoid being detected. When they came to an opening in the trees, he saw a ranch nestled far below the mountain, on the rolling flats to the southeast. Bill Cowan's ranch was a familiar sight, but Whip saw no sign of his horses. He nudged the blue on down the mountain, still careful about concealing his pursuit. Two hours later he rode into the courtyard near the main house.

Cowan was in a corral around back, and he hollered at Whip before he got to the ranch house. Whip turned Bandit Blue toward the corral and dismounted. He tied off on the corral fence and crawled up, surveying the area for his horses or anything that might reveal the presence of the horse thieves. His gaze settled on several familiar horses in a nearby corral.

"Howdy," Cowan said as he pulled a burning iron off the hide of a sorrel horse.

The cowboys in the corral let the horse up, and the next few minutes were spent in getting the ropes off the newly branded animal. Cowan walked over to where Whip sat on the top rail.

"You're pert near too late with them ponies, Whip. I just bought six head off Melvin Stone. How many you got for me?"

Whip eyed the sorrel that he'd ridden for the past three months. The horse belonged to him. Whip slid off the fence and walked over to the horse.

"Hold him a minute," he said softly to Cowan's cowboys.

The men stopped working and allowed Whip to walk around the sorrel. Cowan was right on his heels.

"What's the matter?" Cowan demanded.

"That's my sorrel," Whip said.

Cowan stopped in his tracks and studied Whip, who had turned to face him. The two men eyed each other for a few seconds. Then Cowan said, "You'd better look again, Whip. That's a heck of an accusation."

"The brand's been run in the last couple of days. You can see that, Cowan. That's my brand that's been worked over."

"Whip, I do a lot of cattle business with Mr.

Stone, and he gathered up this herd just a couple of days ago. I'm sure he didn't steal them, but it's possible that he could have bought this horse from the man who stole it from you. Shoot, he had thirty-four head of horses."

"I was relieved of thirty-four head."

"Stone's a U.S. marshal. I can't believe he'd have anything to do with stolen stock. I just don't believe it, Whip. But as sure as the sun's hot, I don't doubt what you've said, either. Your hide's true as any hide I ever swapped dukes with, but I won't put a horse-stealing brand on Stone, either."

"What does he look like?"

"He's kinda towheaded, but leans more toward having a brown noggin. His eyes are brown, and he's not much for size. He looks like a gambler, and he's kinda funny about talking too much. Guess that's the lawman in him, but he sure ain't no horse thief. Why, I've bought heifers from him for years. He's a solid businessman."

"Would you know Brownie if you saw him?" Whip asked.

"Sure would. He crept up on me one night in the moonlight and held me at gunpoint while his bandits rustled off a bunch of my stock. I'd remember the way he breathes if I heard it again."

"This fellow, Melvin Stone, was he with the men moving the horse herd?" Whip asked.

"No, they told me that Stone had told them to come this way, and if I wanted some of the stock, to pick out a half dozen head, and so I did."

"Which way do I look, Cowan?" Whip asked.

"They went east out across the flat, but, Whip, there's twenty men pushing that herd. You'd better hope you don't catch up with them alone if there's gonna be fighting. I'll round up some of my men and go with you. I need to know what's been pulled here."

"No, this is my war. Cowan, I want fifty dollars a head for the six horses you say you bought from Mr. Melvin Stone."

"But I already paid seventy apiece for them!"

"That's your loss, Cowan. You bought stolen stock, and that's your problem. You owe me three hundred dollars since you've already branded them."

Whip crawled up the fence and descended the other side to his roan. He mounted and touched his hat brim as he rested his eyes on Cowan.

"Good day, Cowan," he said softly. He turned Bandit Blue and jogged the horse out of the courtyard with Heck on his heels.

CHAPTER SEVEN

IN the dusk of the evening after he'd left Cowan's ranch, Whip saw a spiraling cloud of dust miles away on the eastern skyline, barely visible in the last rays of the sun. He immediately moved his eyes over the terrain and picked out a path of travel off to the north of the trail taken by the horses. This way he could travel fast and elude Brownie if the man was watching the back trail, which Whip knew he would be doing.

In the evening of the next day, he accidentally ran across the horse herd's trail where it had made a swing northward. The manure was only hours old. He'd caught up with them.

Whip made camp in a wind-washed gully, but didn't build a fire, satisfying himself with jerky for a meal. He called Heck to heel as soon as night settled in, and then he went into the sparse brush to investigate the area on foot.

Only moments later, he located the glow of several campfires less than a half mile away. He knew that now was the most dangerous time in an encounter with Brownie. The man never slept in camp with his men, and often dawdled away the night hours by strolling circles some distance out around the camp.

A yellow glow brightened the eastern horizon, and within minutes, the silver of an almost full moon appeared in the sky. This was a stroke of bad luck. The flatlands would be illuminated like day, and Whip had no desire to try to outmaneuver Brownie in the dark, because the man was like a cat.

He returned to his horse, broke camp, and relocated it about a mile back in a dried streambed where his campfire could not be seen easily. He allowed himself a small fire for coffee.

The flames barely licked inches high, but being alone around even the smallest of campfires had a melancholy effect on Whip. Jessica came to his mind, and he let her memory tease him far into the night. Before snuggling down to sleep, he reprimanded himself:

She's a grand girl, but you're a fool, Whip Cordeen. Some young cowboy of Jasper's is gonna win her heart, and if you keep this up, you're gonna end up with a heartache. You're too old for her, so your best bet is to forget it.

Before the rays of the morning sun flooded the land, Whip gained the summit of one of several high bluffs and tied his horse out of sight. He lay down on his stomach, wiggled to the edge of the reddish rock, and located the horse herd below. But they were too far in the open to rescue.

Close to two dozen outlaws lolled around on bedrolls. Some were sitting down in the dirt, and Whip assumed they were playing cards. They were waiting for something. Late afternoon found Whip still keeping a watch below and unable to come up with a plan that would balance the odds. Heck suddenly growled from beneath the shade of a nearby bush where he could escape the heat of the sun.

Whip turned his head and, following the dog's eyes, he saw a man standing back from the edge of a nearby bluff, waving his arms. Whip tensed and thought himself discovered, but realized that the man was waving at him and then toward the back side of the bluff where he sat.

Whip responded like a bullet jacked from a chamber. He wiggled around and stayed low to keep from being seen from below. Then he got to his feet far back from the cliff edge. Returning to Bandit Blue, he felt his blood race when he saw the horse throw its head up and prick its ears down toward the back side of the bluff where they'd come up. The bluff was not large enough to hide a man going down from a man coming up. Whip pulled out the carbine and waited, barely fifty feet from the trail.

Within minutes, a Ute rode his mount into view. Just when Whip felt sure the Indian wasn't going to notice his presence, he jerked his horse to a stop and studied the tracks on the ground. Squinting like a cougar, the Ute slowly pivoted his head, searching the area. Though Whip was hidden well, the Ute's trained eye locked on him. The Ute grinned and spoke a word in his own language as he threw a leg over his pony's neck and slid to the ground with his rifle in hand. Whip didn't understand the Ute language, but the man's manner removed any doubt of the fact that he intended a hand-to-hand battle.

Whip obliged him and stepped out of the brush with his carbine. The Ute eyed him mutely for a moment, then set his long-barreled weapon against a rock and pulled a knife. Whip answered the challenge and set his carbine carefully against the base of a brush. But he left his bowie in the scabbard on his belt. He preferred to have his fists free.

Most Indians were wrestlers of some merit and their ability to kick with their feet was not foreign to Whip's knowledge, but fistfighting was not one of their skills. The combatants half crouched several yards from each other. Then the Ute moved in so quickly, slicing with the knife, that Whip barely avoided a fatal wound. He felt blood on his shirt, but didn't look down. He circled slowly, letting his hands hang half curled at his sides. Again the Ute moved like a striking snake, but Whip threw up a guard arm and knocked him aside, and then planted a fist right into his nose. The Ute went down, but before Whip could pounce on him, he was back on his feet, shaking away numbness with a toss of his head.

Now the Ute paid strict attention to Whip's fists. He sprang in twice more, missed Whip with his knife, but also managed to elude Whip's swift hands. They circled several more times. Then Whip faked a punch. The Ute dodged, but Whip managed to deliver a neck-breaking punch to his face. He followed up with an uppercut that caught the Ute before he had recovered totally from the first blow.

Knocked cold, the Ute sank to the red dirt while Whip followed through and dropped to his knees, straddling the young man's body. He raised his powerful arms and started to deliver a double-fisted blow to the Ute's throat. Then he hesitated with upraised hands.

He slowly lowered his hands and stared at the Indian. Common sense told him that he'd be safe only if the Indian was dead, but he got to his feet and declined doing what he had the power to do.

He quickly cut the leather thong that held the Indian pony's blanket in place on its back, and tied the Ute's hands with it. Next, he tied it high and tight to a stout bush. He cut the blanket and gagged him.

"Here, Heck, watch him," Whip commanded, and waited as the dog positioned himself a yard or so from the Indian.

After tying the pony so that it couldn't run off to the herd below, Whip turned his attention to the far bluff. He couldn't see the man who had waved the warning to him earlier. He wondered if Cowan had followed in spite of his telling him not to.

He wiggled to the edge and looked down. Two new riders were in camp. One was Brownie, and the other, a short sturdy man, had just stepped off a stocking-legged, bald-faced sorrel. A brief discussion ensued; then Brownie mounted and loped his horse out of sight down the dry wash. Whip felt a surge of anger as the outlaw leader slipped away. Brownie was the man he wanted.

Whip stilled his anger and put his mind on getting his horses. If the man on the far bluff was Cowan, he'd probably help him with the horse thieves. By shooting and then moving quickly to different positions on the bluff, they might be able to make the men below believe that a big gang of ambushers was above them. If that worked, the outlaws would scatter.

Suddenly Whip saw Brownie again. The silver conchas on the gear on the black horse reflected blindingly in the summer sun. Halfway up the back side of the far bluff, Brownie had his rifle leveled across the saddle at something below the summit of the bluff.

Whip knew his target had to be the man who had waved the warning. He quickly drew a bead with the carbine and hoped the weapon would carry the distance. But before he could pull the trigger, the repercussion of Brownie's weapon bounced off the surrounding bluffs. Whip fired. He saw Brownie scramble into the saddle, then plunge his horse on around the turn of the incline and disappear from sight. His mind working rapidly, Whip used the shot from Brownie's rifle to help in his charade. He began pumping shells through his carbine to the men below. He pulled his revolver and fired a couple of rounds. Then he leaped back to where the Ute's rifle lay propped against the rock and shot a few rounds from a different position. After reloading the carbine and revolver, he peered over the edge. The outlaws were saddling, but those that were mounted were already hazing the horse herd in a stampede out across the flats. Whip watched them go, then sent several more rounds into the valley below.

Suddenly Heck growled, and Whip saw that the dog was looking down, not at the Ute but at Brownie, who was working his way up the bluff they were on. He leveled the carbine, but just as he squeezed the trigger, Brownie realized his error and spun the black off into the protection of the gullies below. The outlaw disappeared, and minutes later, Whip saw a thin spiral of dust kicking up out of the riverbed a mile to the west. Brownie was leaving the trouble behind.

When Whip gazed over the edge of the bluff, the valley was empty. He had lost his horses. He turned back toward the Ute. The man was now wide-awake, staring eyeball to eyeball with Heck as the dog twitched his lips in a snarl and showed his sharp teeth. The Ute cast a confused look at Whip. Plainly, he was surprised to be alive. Suddenly tired, Whip heaved a loud sigh and walked over to the Indian. He cut the man free of his bonds, then roughly got him to his feet. He knew the man had to understand English if he was riding for Brownie.

"Go!" he yelled.

The Ute untied his horse and mounted it in a single leap. He looked back at Whip, then turned the horse and streaked off the bluff as if an evil spirit were in pursuit.

Whip stashed the Ute's carbine and knife in a bush, because he had no place to carry extra weapons. He mounted Bandit Blue and slowly descended to the valley floor. After crossing it, he climbed up the bluff where Brownie had shot at something. A short while later, he saw a chestnut horse tied to a scrub brush. He maneuvered the roan around the chestnut and continued up the bluff. Dismounting, he searched the rocks where Brownie had been aiming his rifle.

He ducked under a low-hanging ledge, then stumbled over a booted foot that stuck out from a boulder. He looked down and grimaced at the man who was more than a mere acquaintance. He was U.S. Deputy Marshal John Wilhelm.

Whip dropped to his knees and inspected the ring of blood that saturated the man's shirt. The man was shot high in the back, but he was still alive. Carefully Whip lifted Wilhelm to his shoulders and made his way back to where the chestnut was tied. He put the lawman across his saddle and tied him down with the lariat. Then he gathered up the reins of the chestnut, mounted Bandit Blue, called to Heck, and headed back toward Cowan's ranch.

In the two days of travel back to the cattle ranch, John Wilhelm didn't regain consciousness. He remained in a delirium, and groaned and screamed almost continuously. Whip managed to feed him a broth made from rabbit meat. He had thought about trying to dig out the lead, but the wound was deep, beyond his ability.

The morning of the third day, Whip rode into the courtyard with the unconscious lawman. Cowan came on the run and immediately sent one of his men for the doctor in Magpie Springs. With the help of his cowboys he put Wilhelm to bed inside his rambling house. Whip stayed only long enough to drink some coffee and stuff down a large chunk of beef roast. Then he went out to the hitching rack and untied the roan.

"Where'd you and the marshal meet up?" Cowan asked.

"How'd you know who he is?"

"He came riding in here just hours after you left. He said he was on the same trail as you."

"Did you tell him about your U.S. marshal friend, Stone?"

"No. Should I have?"

"I reckon," Whip answered.

"Well, I just told him which way you and the herd went. I figured if he wanted to know anything, he'd have asked me."

"You could have offered the information in view of the circumstances, and since it had to be plumb evident he was a stranger and wouldn't know to question you."

"I think you're wrong to suspect Stone. Sorry you didn't find your horses," Cowan grumbled.

"I found them," Whip told him.

"Why didn't you bring them back?"

"Because . . . by the way, Cowan, what color horse does your friend Melvin Stone ride?"

"Stocking-legged, bald-faced sorrel."

"Because," Whip continued coldly, "Stone came riding into the outlaw camp with Brownie. A bit later the shooting started, and the last I saw of my horses, they were hightailing it for Kansas, from the looks of things." Whip swung into the saddle, but continued to look Cowan in the face as he did so. He studied the rancher a minute longer, then spoke:

"You ought to be more careful about your friends, Cowan. When you've got my money, leave it with Jasper Hunt."

Whip nodded good-bye, then turned the roan and jogged out of the courtyard. Cowan was a good man, but he'd been hornswoggled for sure, and Whip wondered if the heifers Cowan had been buying for years from Stone weren't the ones that Brownie had stolen from him.

When Whip rode into Jasper Hunt's front yard, Ty was sound asleep in the coolness of the covered, open-air porch. Whip left Bandit Blue and Heck at the barn and ambled up to the main house with the intention of rousing Ty, but his partner looked so peaceful that he couldn't summon up enough orneriness to wake him. He pulled a chair a foot or so from the wall and placed it next to Ty, then sat down and leaned back until the back touched the wall. He closed his eyes, pulled his hat down to his nose, folded his arms across his chest, and let his feet dangle as he drifted off into a much-needed, peaceful sleep.

Jasper and Jessica rode into the courtyard in the early afternoon. Jasper didn't take notice of Whip up on the porch, and after Jessica had dismounted, he took her horse to the barn.

Upon the porch, Jessica pulled off her hat and slapped it against her riding skirt to rid it of dust. Seeing Whip, she trembled in relief that he had returned. Somehow, the absence of the man had made her memory of him grow with each day.

She advanced toward him, halting only inches away. She wanted to speak to him, to see his face and hear him talk, but to disturb him seemed unkind. She continued to stand beside him, just satisfied to be near him. Finally, one of his arms untwined itself from the other, and then his hand reached for his hat, grasped it by the brim, and removed it from his face in one swift sweep. His eyes were penetrating into hers intensely, yet curiously.

"Oh, I'm sorry I disturbed you, Mr. Cordeen. I did wake you, didn't I?"

"No, I woke up when the horses came into the yard."

"Then you saw me come up the stairs by peeking out from under your hat?"

He nodded, and his penetrating eyes caused her to look away. She fumbled with her hat.

"I'm so glad you returned safely. Mr. Wilhelm said he feared you had taken on too much."

She let her eyes travel across his face and down his shirt, as if verifying his safe return. When her attention focused on the dried blood on his shirt, she saw the half-healed knife wound through the hole in it.

"You've been hurt!" she cried.

The devil on Whip's shoulder took over again. He let his expression grow lax, and he sighed heavily.

"Yes, Jessica, I've been through a torture. I was stabbed by a wild savage, and then my life's blood almost drained plumb out of me. I had to crawl most of the way back here 'cause I was too weak to get up on my horse. That big, old, clumsy roan horse kept stepping all over my carcass, and I'm plumb stomped to death. I may not make it until morning. I've about used up all my strength."

"Oh, Whip!" she moaned, and slipped a soft hand on each side of his face.

Whip put his hand behind her head, and his eyes seemed to pull her like a magnet. When their lips met, he kissed her softly, then pressed her face against his cheek.

"Oh, you poor man," she whispered.

"That's the most gosh-awful, long-winded tale I ever heard out of you, Whip Cordeen," Ty growled in disgust.

Jessica drew back, her eyes blinking rapidly. She stared from Whip to Ty and then back to Whip. Suddenly her cheeks flushed with anger.

"You fiend! You did it again! Have you no shame, no honor? I'll never believe you again!" she cried, and quickly ran through the door, almost knocking down Mrs. Valez in her desperate escape.

Mrs. Valez said to Whip as she walked onto the porch, "You like Miss Hunt. That is good."

Whip grinned and tipped his chair back on its legs. He replaced his hat and stretched. "I've never said that," he told her.

"You didn't need to. It shows," she said.

"Maybe you don't see as well as you think." Whip turned on Ty. "The next time I'm talking to a lady, you keep your comments to yourself."

"Cracky, pard, one more minute and she'd have kissed you again, and I couldn't have stood that."

"And why is that?" Whip asked.

" 'Cause I wish it was me. Criminy, Whip! This whole outfit of Jasper's, including me, has fallen plumb in love with that little gal. I can't see why she keeps letting herself be roped in by your awful lies."

"We're both too old for her, so you've fallen plumb in love in vain," Whip said.

"I am not. I'll never be too old."

"Well, pard, I'm gonna keep on harvesting all the sweetness I can steal, because real soon one of Jasper's young punchers will lay claim on her for good."

Mrs. Valez looked at the wound in Whip's side. "You come inside immediately," she said. "That needs to be cleaned and bandaged."

"I've had it several days. It'll be all right."

"No, *señor,* you come now. I have seen these things take a strong man to the grave. Come, I will not allow you to kill yourself."

Whip allowed himself to be hauled to his feet and pulled into the house. A half hour later he was no longer arguing with the wisdom of the comely housekeeper. The wound was infected more than he had guessed. He didn't offer any argument, either, when she said he needed rest, and he followed her to a bedroom. He had barely gotten in bed when Jessica and Jasper came into the room.

"Sleeping in the middle of the day?" Jasper asked, taking a teasing poke at Whip.

"Doctor Valez's orders."

"Can you tell me what happened before you conk out?"

Whip related the events to Jasper, and also told him about Melvin Stone. They discussed things that had happened recently with the stolen cattle, and tried to come up with answers that could tie Stone and Brownie together.

"Maybe Stone doesn't know what Brownie is,

and is doing business with him on the up and up," Jasper suggested.

"No, if he's a marshal, he knows everything about Brownie."

"There's got to be a way we can put a stop to Brownie and his crimes."

"He's not a man you can pursue without getting your feathers singed, and he'll slip away while he's doing it," Whip pointed out. "He's got to be trapped. We've got to come up with a plan to lure him out, and I don't know what we could think of that he'd be fool enough to fall for. Even at that, in the final moments, the only way he will go down for good is in a gunfight."

"Well, we sure ain't got the funds to hire a gunfighter, and even if we did, I ain't so sure there's but one or two who could beat Brownie. I've seen him draw, and I sure don't want nothing to do with a gunfight with that man."

"Wouldn't be a picnic," Whip muttered.

"Is there anything I can do for you?" Jessica asked, her face still red here and there.

Whip wished Jasper wasn't there, so that he could tell Jessica to stay and hold his hand and kiss him to sleep.

"Just see that Bandit Blue and Heck are cared for. I sure hate to leave a horse stalled, but I'm gonna get some sleep."

Early the next morning, Jessica knocked softly at Whip's door, peeked in, saw him still sawing logs, closed the door softly, and tiptoed away. An hour later, after breakfast was over, she strolled down to the barn in the morning sunshine. Mrs. Valez was there, tying up her buggy horse.

"Why do you ride so early?" Jessica asked.

"It's the most peaceful time, and the beginning of a day I will never live again. I like to greet it. It makes life not so alone."

Jessica walked over to where the blue roan hung his head out over the top rail of a box stall. She reached out and touched his head, stroking it firmly. The horse lowered his head and leaned into her petting.

Mrs. Valez said, "That horse likes women. Perhaps his owner was a woman before Brownie made off with him."

"I wonder. . . . He sure is tickled to see me, and he's never really seen me before," Jessica said.

"Put a halter on him and take him for a walk. A horse was meant to run free. Confining one is cruelty. He'll enjoy the walk. Go ahead," Mrs. Valez urged.

Jessica haltered the horse easily, then led it out into the morning sunshine. She noticed the cowboys looking at her, and she wondered at their looks, but she continued leading Bandit Blue to a grassy spot where he could graze. She sat down and let him have all the rope he wanted. After a while the horse stopped cropping the grass and came and stood over her, switching at flies. Jessica scratched

Heck behind the ears as the dog flopped over on his back and tried to devour all her attention.

Jessica looked at a nearby stump and then at Bandit Blue's back. She couldn't resist slipping up on the blue silk. Leading the horse over to the stump, she climbed up on it and then slid across to his back. She nudged the horse forward on a loose rope, and Bandit Blue walked out as if he'd carried her bareback every day of his life. Jessica rode him that way for over an hour, then turned the horse back toward the ranch. As she jogged the roan through the courtyard, she heard murmurings from the cowboys, and some even took off their hats and gaped like she had done some admirable feat. Surely they'd seen a girl ride a horse bareback with a halter before.

She turned Bandit Blue loose in the corral with the halter on, dragging the rope. She made her way to the house for a cup of coffee and another flapjack covered with preserves.

The cowboys ambled over to the corral and discussed what they had just seen. A man called Wren belittled Jessica's ride, and he got a few hot comments from the other cowboys. Wren was unpopular because of his mean disposition, but he was a good cowboy and therefore the men tolerated him. Suddenly he stalked away from the group and came back toting his saddle. He stepped through the gate with it, then caught up Bandit Blue.

"I wouldn't try that," warned a cowboy who had seen Whip knocked out on the roan's back.

"You're all a bunch of sissies. If that female can ride this roan hide, I sure can, and I'm tired of hearing you fellers oh and ah over Whip Cordeen riding him like he was some kind of champion broncobuster or something." Roughly, Wren threw the saddle on Bandit Blue's back, and then he jerked the cinch up savagely.

Bandit Blue curled his nostrils ominously, and a warning smolder burned in his intelligent eyes. He rolled his back slightly under the sheepskin and waited for the man to mount. The hackamore came next. Then Wren blindfolded Bandit Blue's eyes just to be safe.

"Wren, I wouldn't do that," another cowboy warned. "That's Whip Cordeen's horse, and he's gonna be mad as the devil. You better stop while you're ahead."

"I don't lose sleep over the likes of Cordeen," Wren answered, then stuck his foot in the stirrup and stepped aboard. He bent forward and took up a short rein on one side, then whipped off the blind.

Bandit Blue waited for the man to turn him. Wren laughed as the horse stood quietly on all fours.

"You fellers have been buffaloed. This is a nag."

Wren tugged on the rein to turn the horse in a circle. Bandit Blue came around like a whirlwind and bolted toward the heavens. Wren lost a lot of leather and was almost unseated when the horse catapulted straight upward, but he managed to scramble back into the seat when the blue leveled off. The downward plunge was like opening the drop on a gallows. Down, down they went, swifter and swifter as best Wren could tell, and then they connected with solid earth. Wren crumpled like a rag doll and failed to be in the saddle when Bandit Blue swooped upward again. Wren was not unconscious, but he was hurt. He tried to stand as Bandit Blue trotted over to the far side of the corral and watched him. Wren stood up and tried to take a step, but he wobbled and fell. "Criminy!" he muttered as his world whirled dizzily.

Suddenly Jessica ran through the gate and over to the horse. Bandit Blue shied slightly but held his ground. She quickly stripped the saddle and hackamore from the horse and led it by the halter.

"How dare you!" she said to Wren as she passed him.

At the gate, she came face-to-face with Whip. His eyes were horribly cold and didn't seem to see her. She touched his arm and implored with her eyes, but he wouldn't look at her. His attention was totally on Wren.

"Whip, don't fight, please. It's over," she said.

"No, it isn't," he whispered. "Take Bandit Blue to the barn."

Jessica hurried away with the horse. She glanced over her shoulder and saw Whip walk to within several feet of Wren.

Whip looked down at Wren like the god of war

and thunder about to unleash a frightening storm. He spoke so softly the men on the fence barely heard him.

"You tried to ride my horse?"

"I reckon I tried, but I found out he's what they said," Wren answered.

"Why?" Whip demanded quietly.

"Because that Eastern, high-minded female has ideas that don't fit out here. She's trying to destroy us men's manhood by besting us at our trade. She was just lucky, that's all."

Whip's eyes narrowed to slits, and he had to suppress an urge to take a swing at Wren. In his present state of mind, he would probably break the man's neck.

"Wren," he said, "any time a man's manhood is threatened by the talents of a woman, that man had better take another look at his manhood."

Not a man on the fence dared breathe. Whip had insulted Wren beyond what any man but a coward could take without retaliation. Wren was fast with a gun, and they all waited tensely, expecting him to go for it, but Wren hesitated, glancing at the way Whip's gun hung.

Whip continued when Wren made no move to answer the challenge: "You pick up your hat, and pick up your saddle and your horse out of the remuda. You're through here."

"You're not the boss man, Cordeen," Wren muttered.

"I'm the man who told you to move on, and you better get going," Whip said.

Wren fidgeted for a minute, then picked up his hat from the dust. He crammed it on his head, gave Whip a weasely look, and went over to his saddle. He bent and picked it up with his left hand, then walked back across the corral. He continued on past Whip, but just before he got to the gate, he turned and let his saddle drop in the dust. His right hand slipped down near his gun butt.

Whip had pivoted as Wren passed, and he was watching him like a hawk. He saw Wren take the stance of a gunfighter.

"Wren," Whip said softly, but Wren and everybody else heard, "don't draw on me unless you want to die!"

Wren paled and bit his lip. He studied Whip uncertainly, then slowly reached down for his saddle again. At that moment Jasper stepped through the gate and got between Whip and Wren.

"He don't have the authority to fire me, Jasper. I've been a darn good cowboy for you," Wren said.

"Yup, I don't disagree with you, Wren. But I wouldn't keep a horse with a disposition like yours, and I ain't gonna keep you. No man runs a woman down on this ranch, and you better ride far enough that the gossip that comes from here don't catch up to you. Now git!"

Wren got his horse out of the remuda, saddled up, and rode away at a gallop. It took several minutes for the fire to leave Whip's eyes, and then he strode past Jasper and started toward the house.

"Where are you going?" Jasper called out.

"Back to bed," he answered without turning as he walked.

Ty closed the gate as Jasper stepped through, gazing thoughtfully after Whip.

"You know, Ty," the rancher muttered, "I don't think Whip was bluffing Wren. I believe he can shoot and shoot fast."

"I know Whip pretty well, Jasper," Ty said, "and he wasn't bluffing a bit."

CHAPTER EIGHT

WHIP spent the next few days working for Jasper Hunt. Often they discussed ways to pull Brownie into the open, but nothing of any value presented itself. Ty and Whip argued about building a new cabin, but they could agree on nothing.

Jessica was puzzling to Whip. She seemed to watch him all the time, but when he tried to speak to her, she became elusive. He knew he was the envy of all the cowboys because he had managed to appropriate two kisses from the lady, and none of them had even held hands with her. The thought of becoming romantically involved with Jessica Hunt never really crossed his mind, because he knew there wasn't a chance of such a happening. He saw her as Jasper's pretty daughter, a friend, and yet, on the other hand, an intriguing woman whose irritation and embarrassment at his pranks brought him hours of amusement.

It was late afternoon when Whip pulled the saddle off a mustang that had managed to throw Jasper's cowboys over and over. The horse had caused

Whip some worry a couple of times, but had not unloaded him. He turned the speckled gray loose in a large corral with several others, then hauled his saddle across the enclosure and threw it up on the top rail of the fence. Jasper and Ty were sitting nearby, and Whip crawled up and sat down close to them.

"Got a message from down Cowan's way," Jasper said. "John Wilhelm is gonna stay among the living. Cowan said he ought to be headed back up this way by tomorrow."

"Guess I better head home," Whip said.

"How come you're avoiding him?" Ty asked. His eyes traveled shrewdly back and forth across Whip's face.

"Why do you avoid Reams?" Whip answered back.

Ty slowly rubbed his healing fingers against one another and put his attention on them as he pondered his answer. "I made a mistake once, but Wilhelm don't care," he mumbled.

"I made a mistake once too," Whip said bitterly. "But Wilhelm *will* care about that, and I'd rather not bump into him."

"Does he know you?" Jasper asked quietly.

"Yes! Now drop it!"

Whip settled his gaze out across the flats. There was a long silence between them, broken only by ranch sounds that played pleasantly on their ears. Suddenly the drum of running hooves caused the three men to look up at the riders who were approaching hurriedly. They were six of Jasper's cowboys, and they slid their horses to a stop next to the fence.

Old Rusty, one of Jasper's oldest and most reliable hands, cried out, "We've got trouble! Boss, them steers we gathered for the Army fort over by Meeker were rustled off yesterday. We followed them most of the night, and then, this morning, we found them in a canyon thirty miles west of here. There wasn't a rustler around, but we were beat and out of grub. Since the herd was scattered like grass seed in a tornado, we figured we'd come back and get some food and some help to round them up."

"Just abandoned?" Jasper said incredulously.

"Yup, just like the others."

"I'll be hog-tied. Don't make no sense. Rest up, you men, then grab as many hands as you think you'll need and get them back here." Jasper turned to Whip as the men dismounted and unsaddled their horses. "What do you make of that? That's twice now."

"Maybe this isn't just twice," Whip said softly. "Maybe the rustled cattle were in such small numbers that nobody followed them far, and maybe now that the herd numbers are getting up around thirty or forty, you're following them because it's beginning to pain you."

"Well, that's pretty close to right. We've only followed these last two rustlings to any distance. What have you got on your mind?"

"I think Brownie runs them only far enough to lose your interest in chasing them. Then he leaves them until things cool down, returns later, and gathers up the cattle and herds them somewhere else, unpursued. It wouldn't matter to him if he lost a hundred head in the brush. He didn't have any cattle to start with, so even one old cow would be to his gain."

"That could be, Whip, but it don't make any sense to drive only thirty head clear to the railhead."

"No, it don't, so he's got to have a place he's holding them. Then he has a prearranged sale, or else he'd get the attention of the inspectors if he ran a large herd of run brands through the stockyard. I'll lay odds that Brownie is just a feather in a bigger buzzard."

"That goes along with what Wilhelm was hinting on," Jasper said thoughtfully. "He also said that Brownie made a mistake before, when he tried to move into a section of Kansas, by not cleaning out any men that would fight him. Maybe Brownie has decided to use this range as a holding area for stolen cattle, and the reason he stole your horses was to get you out somewhere and waylay you, Whip. He's smart enough to have learned by now that you'd be a threat to something like that, and he sure couldn't ride in and shoot you in bed, because he'd get hunted till hell froze over. A murder like that can be proved, but it would be anybody's guess who was guilty out there in the flats somewhere."

Whip thought for a few minutes. Then he came up with a plan.

"Jasper, I know you have a delivery date on those steers, but I think this overrides any other need. Instead of bringing those steers back, leave them be. That's the very bait we've been looking for. I'll leave this afternoon, and you send as many men as you can, a few at a time. It'll look like circle riders, so Brownie won't suspect anything if he's watching the area. We'll all just gather quietly, then hunker down under a tree, and wait for the outlaws to return and gather up the herd. Handled right, we could cut the heart out of this band of rustlers."

Jasper considered it for only seconds. He grunted as he climbed off the fence. "Take the reins, Whip. Use as many men as you need, and take anything from here you need. I'll tag along for the ride."

Whip saw Jessica coming from the house. As usual, the sight of her golden hair falling down across her shoulders caused a strange warmth in his heart.

"Jasper, you stay with Jessica. I can't promise the outcome of this, and she needn't be left alone in this world."

"I don't plan on getting killed, and I didn't remember asking for a guarantee on life from anybody. As far as Jessica is concerned, well, she wouldn't be alone if it came to that. Her mother is back East."

"You told me to take the reins, Jasper, and first off, I said for you to stay here!" Whip said. He jumped off the fence and reached up and snugged his hat down like he would before a wild ride on a bronc. Ordering Jasper around could cause all-out war. "See you when I get back."

"You'll see me when I choose, mister, and I go where I please!"

Jessica came up to the fence and peered in. She saw that Whip and her father were not in agreement about something and kept silent. Jasper glared at Whip and at Jessica too, just because she was there when his temper was flaring. Then he stomped out of the corral.

Whip reached through the corral poles and put firm hands on her shoulders. She started to twist out of his grip, then saw the stern look in his eyes.

"What is it, Whip?" she asked.

"You haven't told him about your mother."

"No, I just haven't been able to. He's been so happy, Whip. I just can't tell him."

"You must. It's time. Don't let him go with me."

Whip allowed his eyes to linger on her. He felt a pain touch somewhere deep in his heart, and he let go of her abruptly. He made for the house to pack food and a carbine. Twenty minutes later he cantered his powerful roan out across the grasslands and started the rugged climb up the mountains to the west of the ranch. Heck darted happily on both sides, hunting squirrels as he followed the big roan horse.

Inside the house, Jessica strolled to the kitchen, hoping to find Mrs. Valez, but her father was there too, packing food into a saddlebag. Mrs. Valez was wrapping staples and handing them to him.

Jessica took a deep breath and fortified herself for the unpleasant task at hand. She stepped forward and gazed somberly into her father's questioning eyes, only inches from hers.

"Jessica, I have to pack," he said, and reached down to remove her hand from the bags.

"Whip said for you not to go."

"Whip don't tell me what to do!" Jasper exploded. "He's worried I might get done in out there and that it would leave you alone. That's all there is to his blasted orders. It ain't gonna happen, and you wouldn't be left alone, so forget what Whip said."

Jasper moved her hand, but Jessica returned it and held the flap shut. Then she slipped her arms around him and buried her face against his chest. He clasped her tightly.

"Here, here, what's the matter?"

"Mother passed away. This is home."

She felt him tremble, and his arms went limp though they stayed around her. She couldn't look at him.

"No," he whispered, "that can't be. I'm waiting . . . I've waited a lifetime. She was gonna come home. . . . Jessie, she's coming, isn't she?" Jasper put his fingers under her chin and forced her to look into his eyes. "She's coming, isn't she?" he whispered again, nodding his head affirmatively in desperate need for that answer.

"No, Father," she whispered. Seeing the tears in his eyes, she buried her face against his shirt again.

Jasper gently pushed her away from him. He stared at her, shaking his head back and forth.

"I've waited . . . no, she has to come home. . . ."

He released her. The skin on his face trembled and his cheeks became wet, but he held his ground, refusing to turn and run from what he had heard, though all his inner being screamed for him to escape. He needed to sit, but there was no chair close, so he steadied himself against the table with outstretched arms, his head bowed. He forced himself to accept what he had learned. His dream, the dream that had given him the desire to fight and overcome, suddenly existed no longer. She was gone.

"Whip knew about this?" he said in a husky voice, looking up at Jessica.

"Yes."

Jasper turned to Mrs. Valez, who stood near the table, tears streaming down her cheeks at his heartache. She wanted to go over and comfort him, but it was not her place. She was as firm in her ways as he was in his.

"Tina, unpack my bags," he said softly. He reached out a hand to Jessica. "Come, Jessie, tell me all the good things I have missed. She did plan to come home, didn't she?"

Hands clasped, Jasper and Jessica walked through the house that he had built for the woman who would never walk its spacious hallways. Much later, they walked out onto the porch, still hand in hand. They descended its steps and strolled out toward the flatlands beyond the ranch.

Whip watched the edge of trees on the far side of a meadow. Several spotted cows and a few brindles grazed peacefully, unaware of the presence of the eighteen cowboys who blended in with the shadows in the timber. Near the upper point of the meadow, two more of his men curled down behind a jagged outcropping of rocks. There were four more cowboys stationed along the face of the mountain slope, on the lookout for riders from the valleys. Whip turned to Ty, who sat nearby in the crook of a hollow tree.

"I wish you had stayed at the ranch," Whip said.

"Well, I didn't. I'm tired of being sick."

"You haven't regained the use of your fingers yet, pard, so stay behind me when the shooting starts. You should've stayed at the ranch."

"You already said that, and you've said it so darn many times I think I'll stuff your mouth full of pine needles if you say it again," Ty threatened.

"Your experience with Brownie hasn't affected your mouth," Whip teased.

Ty grinned and put his attention on the meadow.

He watched it for a while, then put his gaze on the blue sky overhead. "You know what would bother me about having somebody throw dirt in my face?" he said.

"Huh? You mean when they plant you?" Whip asked.

"Yeah. I always hated getting dirt in my teeth when I got throwed off a bronc into the corral dust. It bothers me to think I might have to chew dirt all the way to heaven. If you're around when I answer the call, please put my hat over my mouth," Ty said.

"You got my word on it, pard."

"What would you want me to do for you?" Ty asked.

"Take care of my dog and my cat and give my horse to Jessica," Whip said.

"Ain't there anything that bothers you about being stuck in a cold hole in the ground?"

"No. I figure that by that time I won't care."

"Well, I would. I've had to bury a few men, and I think they knew what was going on, but just couldn't say nothing. If I see you standing there letting dirt get in my teeth, I'll ask the Big Boss to let me come back and haunt you over it."

The sun reached high noon, then began its lazy slide into the western sky. Whip and Ty perked up as a cowboy came riding toward them under the cover of the trees. He pulled his mount up when he saw them, then urged the horse forward.

"Jehoshaphat!" he exclaimed as he halted his horse again. "For a minute it didn't look like you. Whip, there's a good-sized body of men flushing the brush below the rimrocks. We saw two smaller groups break off and head out in a wing, driving cattle. They're gathering stock, and, Whip, I saw that fancy black horse and its rider watching them from a high point. Brownie isn't mixing with his men."

"Keep your eyes sharp, and every one of you that can, fight back-to-back so you don't get it between the shoulder blades. Remember that Brownie will come in behind you. Watch your back!" Whip turned to Ty. "Pardner, I'd rather you hid out here somewhere."

"Nope, I'm coming along. Don't pamper me, Whip. It makes me burn!"

"All right," Whip muttered, then turned back to the cowboy. "Where does it look like the greatest concentration of cattle are?"

"Near the base of the rimrocks."

"We'll start there and dig in. If the situation changes, we'll move with the cattle gathering. Pass the word on that I'll shoot first. Have the men stay hidden until then, if they can. Good luck, cowboy."

Whip and Ty mounted their horses as the cowboy rode off. Like part of the shadows beneath the dense foliage, they slipped quietly through the trees and tied their horses in a hidden spot behind the rimrocks. Then they went on foot. As Whip edged carefully around a jagged outcropping of granite, he saw the rustlers working cattle in and out of the brush below. To his satisfaction, the cattle were being pushed toward the rimrocks in order to use the natural corral as a holding area until the herd was gathered.

Whip kept looking for Brownie. Since the man approached only from the rear, Whip searched for a spot where he could shoot toward the front from the rock fortress while protecting his back from a rear attack. He intended to make Ty stay behind him, out of harm's way. After looking back over his shoulder to where they had tied their mounts, Whip motioned to Ty to stay put, and then he crept along in search of a safe spot. A half hour later he found what he wanted, and had also located several of his men snugged down in the rocks below. Whip returned to Ty and motioned him to follow. Once settled, Whip waited for the rustlers to gather with the rounded-up cattle two hundred feet below.

As the rustlers came into view, talking out loud and herding the cattle, it became evident that they were totally confident and didn't expect an ambush. In fact, they were being careless, as Whip saw it. He drew a bead and waited for more of the outlaws to ride into firing range. Several of his cowboys were sneaking down the back side of a rocky ridge in order to come in from behind and stop the rustlers' escape route. He saw two more outlaws arrive with cattle. They dismounted, and like the others, they seemed to be waiting for a signal to move the cattle out of the ravine.

Whip fired. Pandemonium broke loose below when the rimrocks erupted in a steady roar of gunfire as the cowboys opened fire. Whip grimaced as men fell, and a bitter memory screamed at him from out of the past. He set his jaw, gritted his teeth, and continued to fire at the outlaws below.

He was reloading the carbine, but keeping an eye on what was going on, when he became aware of a dozen men creeping over the crest of the ravine. Brownie had split his gang! Though a lot of them were gathering cattle, just as many were protecting them, which was why they had been so lax. Whip realized that another dozen men or more were probably coming up the back side of the rimrocks and would be shooting down at them. Jasper's men were in for a war, not the simple ambush that Whip had expected. Many cowboys would not ride home. Maybe none of them would.

Suddenly, lead showered down from above and two cowboys fell. Because of his location, Whip could not see behind him or overhead. Now his position had become a disadvantage.

Ty slipped up beside Whip. He studied the situation around them and saw another cowboy throw up his hands and fall down between a couple of rocks.

"What's happened?"

"Brownie outsmarted me, that's what!" Whip muttered angrily. "We're in for it, pard. Get your gun out. You're gonna have to shoot, no matter how bad it hurts your paws. You watch left, I'll take right."

The air had become a steady drone of whistling lead. Three outlaws attempted at various times to storm the cavelike protection of Ty and Whip, who saved two cowboys below from back shots, and a third who was taking on more from the front than he could handle.

Slowly the din began to cease, becoming sporadic and scattered, echoing here and there as the lead ricocheted off the rocks. It became almost totally quiet, and Whip and Ty sweated out the minutes, tensely watching the opening of sunshine on each side of them. Suddenly, a shadow on the far side of the cliff exposed the stealthy slink of a man edging down over the rock above their position. Whip nodded at the shadow and Ty nodded back. Together, they each lunged sideways into the sunshine, fired upward at the man, then leaped back into the protection under the rock. The man fell from the rock overhead into the dirt in front of them.

The minutes dragged. Off and on they heard a shot or a volley of shots near their position. Evidently the outlaws had the cowboys pinned down and were moving in, trying to pick them off one by one. Ty grimaced as he wiggled his fingers, trying to loosen them up. His hands were hurting him something awful, but he didn't complain.

Suddenly a long volley of shots was exchanged. Whip peered below, but was careful to stay out of target range to searching eyes. He saw several outlaws mount and ride swiftly into the timber. A few minutes later he saw another one slink off over the crest of the hill. Apparently the cowboys had tipped the scales in their favor. Whip became braver and risked a better look. He saw cowboys still tucked in behind rocks, but their manner was more like that of men seeking a target than men hiding. Whip stepped farther out of the protection of the rock barrier and slowly edged around an abutment of granite and looked up behind him.

He froze as he came eye to eye with the very Ute he had battled out in the flatlands to the east. The Indian carefully watched Whip's hands on the rifle, then turned his head and looked at something on the other side of the rock outcropping. He looked back at Whip. Either man could have easily shot the other, but neither did so. There was an unspoken truce accepted between them. Again the Ute looked to his left, then back at Whip. His eyes signaled an urgency while he stared unblinking.

Whip understood suddenly, and he dropped to his knees and spun around toward the protected area underneath the rock. Ty was out in the sunshine, looking below. He turned his head at Whip's sudden movement and looked over his shoulder at his partner.

"Looks like they're on the run, Whip. Several of the men have come out from—"

Ty sucked in a gasp of air, then slumped as a shot resounded like a crack of thunder. Whip leaped to

Ty, grabbed him before he sank to the ground, and threw lead into the sunshine on the opposite side of the overhang.

Whip fell to the ground with Ty in his arms. Sick at heart, he trembled while he watched the light leave Ty's eyes.

"Pard . . . where are you . . . ?" Ty's voice seemed to whisper from a long tunnel. Then his eyes went blank and his chest ceased to heave.

Whip buried his head against Ty's chest. His whole body shook as he clutched his friend, straining against the grief in his heart, struggling with the pain of the reality. He tried to continue his vigilance, but the knowledge that Ty had just died in his arms destroyed his ability to fight.

"Lord don't. Not Ty," he whispered desperately.

Whip slowly released his hold on Ty's body, then sat numb and dazed in the sand, staring at his partner's pale face, gently cradling the shoulders of the man in his lap. Time seemed to stand still.

Whip's first realization that the world was still going on around him was the knowledge that a shadow broke the blinding glare of the sunlight reflecting off the granite near the side of the overhang. He felt rather than saw the approach of a cowboy. The man crouched down on his heels near him and Ty.

"Whip . . . are you all right?"

It seemed to Whip that there was a thickness to the immediate area around him that kept him from being able to answer, though he heard. He knew that Ty felt cold to his touch, and that he himself was alive, and yet the truth of it all staggered him out of the ability to talk. He felt himself nod slightly, but he continued to look at Ty.

The cowboy left. Whip had no desire to move, though he knew that sitting on the sand beneath the rock overhand changed nothing. Somehow, moving would sever Ty from his life forever, and at this moment, Ty still seemed to be with him. A long while later the cowboy returned.

"Whip, we've got a grave dug. Do you want us to do it?"

Whip shook his head. He lurched slightly as he stood up with Ty in his arms. He felt awareness slip back into his being as his blood raced life through his limbs.

He followed the cowboy to the top of the rim-rock, then on to the brow of the hill under the shade of the pines. He lowered Ty carefully into the earth where the cowboys had scooped out the dirt. But he couldn't let go of his friend.

"I can't put him in that cold hole," he whispered.

Several men came quickly and took Ty out of his arms. Whip backed up and allowed them to do the burial. As they began shoveling dirt into the hole with their hands, Whip suddenly threw up an open palm and stopped them. He slowly removed his hat, wiped the dirt from Ty's face, and placed his hat over it. He carefully put dirt on the hat to hold it in place, then moved back again, motioning to the men to continue. As the dirt went into the hole,

Whip suddenly could take no more, and he turned and strode off. Overhead, the pines gently whispered good-bye to Ty Holden and called Whip into their solitude to help him put himself back together again.

The sun was setting when Whip returned to the mound of earth on the north face of the mountain. He carried a piece of large tree limb in his hands. He stood over the grave only a moment, then forced the limb into the earth. Carved on the limb were the words MY PARD. No more needed to be said about the man who rested there.

Whip looked around and saw the cowboys gathered down in the timber near many more mounds. He made his way down and quietly waited until the men paid their last respects. Then he ordered the cowboys to find their horses and mount up. As soon as they were gathered together, Whip questioned them about what had happened in each of their positions.

"Did anybody see Brownie?" he asked.

"Yeah, we did," two men answered together.

"Where?"

"He was on the west side of your peephole up on the rimrock, and he was scrambling up away from it as fast as he could skedaddle," one of them said.

"There was an Indian up there too," the other man said. "But he was on the east side climbing the rocks. I shot at both of them, but it was a miss both times."

"If you were looking down the rimrock into the ravine, which side would Brownie have been on?" Whip asked.

"Left," they both answered together again.

Whip pondered for a minute. The shot that killed Ty had come from the left side, which meant that Brownic had killed his partner.

Whip knew that Brownie had lost most of his men that afternoon. There was only one thing left for the outlaw to do, and that was to leave the country as fast as he could get the miles behind him. The closest place for supplies was Magpie Springs.

Whip ordered the men to ride to Cowan's ranch, and then he turned Bandit Blue toward Magpie Springs. If Bandit Blue was swift enough, he could catch the outlaw at Magpie Springs when he picked up supplies. If not, Whip vowed, he would follow him to the ends of the earth.

CHAPTER NINE

JOHN Wilhelm jogged his chestnut up to the hitching rack in front of Jasper Hunt's ranch house. He dismounted and nodded a greeting to Jasper and Jessica as they came down the steps to meet him.

"Miss Hunt, I swear that your beauty has increased since I last saw you."

"I'll bet your wife has to beat the ladies from your door when you're home," Jessica said.

"My dear, they never come near my door at home, because there isn't a one that can hold a candle to the beauty of Mrs. Wilhelm."

The trio laughed, then they climbed the steps and sat down at the table on the porch. Wilhelm winced as he sat, but otherwise he didn't show any signs of having escaped death recently.

"Jasper, where are your cowboys? It's as quiet around here as the day before a funeral," Wilhelm said.

Mrs. Valez came out to the doorway, saw their guest, and disappeared inside. She soon returned with cups and the coffeepot. After everyone's cups were filled, she sat down and joined them.

"My men are with Whip. He's come up with a way to catch Brownie, and I think it's a pretty solid bet."

"I saw your man out toward the east," Wilhelm said. "I waved to him out on a bluff, because he was about to get scalped. It wasn't long after that that I got shot. Cowan told me your man gave up chasing after his horses and toted me back instead. A man I've never met saved my life, and you can bet I'm looking forward to meeting him."

Jasper remembered Whip's desire to steer clear of Wilhelm, and declined comment on that statement. "What's your next move?" he asked.

"I'm on my way to Magpie Springs. I found out from Cowan that he's had cattle dealings for several years with a man named Melvin Stone. He said Whip had suspicions that Stone wasn't true blue, but Cowan said he didn't believe it until he got to looking at some heifers Stone had sold him a year ago, and he recognized several that had been stolen from him *two* years ago. Cowan was mad enough to stomp around a campfire and do a war dance on the day I left. Oh, by the way, he told me to give this money to you for this feller named Whip. Guess Cowan bought six horses from Stone that belonged to Whip.

"Anyway, I'm headed for Magpie Springs to send a telegram to the office in Denver. You see, I knew one of the culprits in this ring of thieves, but not the other—until now. Melvin Stone is the connection that's been eluding me. He's a deputy marshal the same as I am, but he's as crooked as a snake tangled in a hammer mill. Brownie has been able to outmaneuver me, obviously because of information he's gotten from Stone. Cowan said he'd testify against him."

Wilhelm accepted a refill from Mrs. Valez, and continued with his conversation:

"I'm gonna work on stopping Brownie out on this end, but the two buzzards he thinks will be waiting for these cattle at the end of the line won't show up. Since your men are gone, Jasper, you don't need to hang around here and boss things. Come on into Magpie Springs with me tomorrow. You and Jessica, and you too, Mrs. Valez. You could all use a trip to town."

"Oh, I'd love that," Jessica said.

"I reckon there's no reason to stay here particularly," Jasper said. "About all I'll do is sit and worry about Whip and my boys. All right, John, we'll make a day of it. It will take most of the day to get there, but if we pull in near suppertime, you can buy us a meal at the boardinghouse. Tina?"

"Yes, Mr. Jasper," she said.

"You will come with us?"

"Thank you, I will go," she said.

Suddenly Wilhelm tensed and turned his ears into the gentle wind. He listened for several minutes, then shook his head.

"I must be hearing things. Sounded like the roar

of a major war there to the southwest. Where'd your men go?" he asked Jasper.

"Southwest," Jasper answered grimly.

They sat quietly on the porch and strained their ears. Every once in a while a faint boom or rumble of booms drifted in on the wind.

"All hell's broke loose," Wilhelm said. "I hope it's Brownie's men and not yours under fire. Blast it! This has gotten out of hand. I think the smartest thing is to request a unit of lawmen out here and clean this up."

"Whip can handle things, John. There ain't no body of ten or twelve lawmen that can do more than Whip leading my cowboys. He knows the country and you don't. Besides, from the sound of things, it's all just about over, anyway. There wouldn't be shooting like that unless Whip was cleaning them out."

"What if Brownie's cleaning out Whip?" Wilhelm said softly.

"If that's happening, Wilhelm, you'd better call in the military, 'cause you got more war than a posse of lawmen are gonna squelch. No, Whip ain't getting whipped. I hope to criminy he ain't." Jasper looked anxiously toward the boom that came to their ears.

It was close to seventy miles from the rimrocks to Magpie Springs. Brownie would have half a day of daylight headstart on Whip. Bandit Blue was surefooted in the darkness, but there was no way

Whip could make the time at night that Brownie could in the daytime. The only time they would be equally matched would be after morning's light. Brownie's black horse was one of the finest in the country, but Whip knew that Bandit Blue was stronger, faster, and bred to run longer. That was his only hope of catching Brownie in Magpie Springs.

Whip rested his animals from near midnight until morning's light. At the crack of dawn, though his sleep had been tortured by nightmares about Ty, Whip continued his pursuit. Near noon, Heck, cut and sore-padded, finally dropped back so far that Whip had to turn around and go pick him up.

In the early afternoon, a ribbon of barren canyons soldiered themselves in formation as they fingered out toward the river east of Magpie Springs. Whip usually came in from the east and missed this maze of rock, but now he had to ride through it from the southwest. He found himself in sparse cedars for a little way, having left the tall timber behind early in the morning. Then the country became almost barren of anything but sage. He tried to map a way through the maze before he dropped down into its depths. Suddenly Bandit Blue threw up his head and walked stiff-legged. Heck growled from his perch across Whip's legs.

Almost like a mirage in the heat waves, the shape of a horse and rider came toward him. The man's weapon was held muzzle downward and the pony was familiar to Whip. The Ute stopped his horse and waited as Whip approached. He stopped his roan a few yards from the Indian. The Indian pointed down into the canyon behind his pony, and then he shook his head. He pointed to a trail that led down into a canyon farther east.

"Brownie?" Whip asked, pointing down the trail he was following.

The Ute shook his head sharply, and pointed far beyond, toward the river. He flapped his arms, signifying a bird. After slapping his shoulders, he pointed to the clouds.

Whip tried to piece it together. Bird, shoulders, and clouds . . . or did the Indian mean "white"? Yes, that was it—the clouds were white. Magpie birds had white on their shoulders. Magpie Springs. This meant that Brownie was still far ahead. Whip pointed down the trail he was on, sure it was the shortest route to the river.

Again the Ute made a negative head motion, but this time he touched his rifle. He turned and pointed to the east trail, then at Whip.

It was as plain as daylight. The trail he was following was an ambush, probably by the few of Brownie's men who had escaped the cowboys. The safe trail was to the east. Why the Ute had befriended him was puzzling to Whip. He had always been led to believe that an Indian took insult when a white man spared his life. The Ute must have valued his life, because he was certainly acting more civilized than the men he rode with. Whip headed the roan toward the eastern trail as the Ute turned his pony and rode down into the canyon to the west.

Whip soon found that the east trail was almost like a cut road. He put Bandit Blue into a swinging lope that ate up the miles. Near the end of the canyon, he saw why the trail was little used. A treacherous stretch of water would be a barrier to most animals, but Bandit Blue had the power to buck the current. Minutes later he leaned forward in the saddle as Bandit Blue clambered up the far bank.

Magpie Springs awaited him as the sun slipped behind a distant ridge. Whip stopped and ordered Heck to get down. He snugged his hat down on his head, set his jaw, and put Bandit Blue into the swinging lope again, swiftly bearing down on the town, now only a mile away.

John Wilhelm and his guests stepped out on the boardwalk. Their appetites were satisfied, but they were worried about Whip and the cowboys. They strolled along as the sun sank behind the rugged skyline in the western sky. Wilhelm always scrutinized the street ahead when he walked a town, and as he did so now, his eyes settled on a black horse tied across the street, down near a panniered packhorse. A slim but strongly built man was stuffing the panniers with supplies. The saddle and strappings on the black horse were adorned with conchas, and John Wilhelm stopped as still as stone when he recognized Brownie loading up for a long journey. Sheriff Reams passed near Brownie, nodded a greeting, and continued on, walking in a stiff manner that clearly showed his fear of the man packing the horse. Brownie laughed as the lawman passed, plainly jeering, challenging the lawman to turn around, but Reams acted as if he didn't hear, and continued walking.

Suddenly Jasper saw Brownie. He quickly put a protective hand on Jessica and Mrs. Valez and shoved them gently inside an open doorway.

"Stay put! There's trouble coming!" he said sternly.

Wilhelm saw Brownie watching him. The outlaw knew the lawman on sight, but showed no fear of him and merely watched him advance slowly along the boardwalk in his direction. The deputy marshal knew he could not outdraw Brownie, but he had taken an oath to protect people and was willing to give his life in the line of duty. He said to Jasper, "Are you with me or am I in this alone? I'd like to know first."

"I'm no gunman, John, but I came into this country to make the place fit to live in, and I'll fight to keep it that way. Count me in."

"He's fast. You'll get only one shot if you get that," Wilhelm said.

"Are you gonna try to start from a place that's got some cover for us?" Jasper asked. He watched Brownie's sly grin as they approached him.

The outlaw knew what they were up to, and he seemed to welcome it. Like a cat sharpening its claws before it sets out to hunt a bird, Brownie pulled his revolver and checked the cylinder. He slid the gun back into the holster and laid his arms across his saddle, watching the men he intended to kill.

Suddenly he looked down the street to the east, where a big roan horse was walking toward him. The horse was barely discernible in the dusk, but Brownie knew who rode the powerful beast. He tensed, shot a look at Wilhelm, then put his attention back on the roan horse.

The tall, dark, hatless horseman looked ghostly in the dimness, coming on like a fearless knight into battle. He rode his horse to a spot about seventy-five feet from Brownie, then turned it into the hitching rack on the outlaw's side of the street. After tying his roan, the rider walked into the street rather than stepping up on the boardwalk, and he advanced challengingly to within twenty feet of Brownie. No words passed as the two men stared each other down, neither wavering beneath the other's gaze.

"It's Whip!" Jasper said.

"It can't be!" Wilhelm gasped. He gaped in disbelief as Whip stood not more than fifteen feet from him, facing Brownie.

"You in this or out of it, Wilhelm?" Brownie demanded softly, still leaning against his horse, directing the question at the marshal but keeping his eyes on Whip.

"I'm out," Wilhelm said loudly.

"You're what?" Jasper sputtered. "Whip needs

help. He ain't no gunman! What do you mean you're out?"

"That ain't Whip anybody. That's Jim Cordeen, and the only one out in that street who needs help is Brownie!"

Brownie knew that Cordeen was fast. He'd faced him before under different circumstances. But the odds had been stacked against Cordeen that time. Now they were equal. Brownie had no doubts in his mind about beating the man to the draw. His worry was Wilhelm. When he shot Cordeen, Wilhelm would be on him like a snake on a gopher.

"Wilhelm, lay your gun down on the walk and step away," Brownie ordered, not changing his position next to the black horse.

"Not a chance, Brownie," Wilhelm said.

"Then you're in," the outlaw said.

"Nope, I'm out."

"Hunt?" Brownie inquired.

"Heck, you know I ain't a threat to you," Jasper said.

"They're both out!" Whip's voice cut the air like lightning out of a cloud, with a wrath that Brownie couldn't miss.

Brownie slowly came around the rump of his horse and stepped out into the street. He cockily walked to within ten feet of Whip, then planted his feet with his arms at his sides, his right palm near his gun butt.

"What's your gripe, Whip?" he asked, his tone friendly but his eyes savage.

"You killed my pardner."

"So . . . ?"

"So I've come to say hi," Whip spat out hatefully.

Brownie barely breathed during the seconds that ticked by, seemingly weighted with lead anchors. Whip appeared almost relaxed. His eyes stared coldly into Brownie's.

"Hi, yourself," Brownie hissed, and reached for his revolver.

Whip Cordeen's arm just seemed to flip at the elbow. Then, almost quicker than speed itself, the deadly iron sprang into his grasp as if it craved to be there, and a bullet ripped a hole through the outlaw's heart and whined on down the street to bury itself in the side of a building.

The shot from Brownie's gun went between Whip's knees and imbedded itself harmlessly into the dirt beyond. The outlaw staggered backward with a shocked, hurt expression on his face. Suddenly he folded at the knees, and his gun slid from his hand. Then he flopped over backward into the street, dead before he landed. A reflection of gold shimmered off a pocket low on his vest.

Whip stood in the street and slowly returned his gun to its holster. He stared at Brownie for only a moment, then walked over to the body and crouched down on one heel. He felt through the man's vest pockets briefly and took something that the onlookers could not identify in the darkness. Then he reached down and picked up Brownie's conchaed hat. After studying it a minute, he tried it on his own head, and appeared to like the fit. Next, he walked over to the black horse and untied its reins. After doing the same to the packed animal, he led the two horses past Brownie's body. He turned his head as he passed the lawman and rancher, but didn't slacken his pace back toward his roan horse.

"Brownie's paying his debts," Whip said.

Wilhelm strode off the boardwalk and crossed the street, following Whip until they stopped near Bandit Blue. Whip turned and faced Wilhelm after he had tied the black's reins to his own saddle.

"Jim! What's the meaning of this? I've thought you dead for twelve years."

"Jim did die twelve years ago," Whip answered softly. "I made a bad mistake and I've corrected it. That's the meaning of this." He untied his reins and started to mount the roan.

"Wait! You're not making sense. What's happened? For heaven's sake, talk to me!"

Whip stared at a few twinkling stars. He wondered if Ty were up there yet or just starting his winged journey. That brought back another memory, and he turned to Wilhelm.

"You sent me to murder, John. I thought I could just ride in and arrest Brownie, but you knew it wouldn't be that way. You figured this fast piece of iron on my hip would clean them out. You had faith in this gun and death. That's all you cared about. I did it, I murdered men to stay alive, but when it was all over, I walked back through that massacre and saw that four were boys, not hardened outlaws. I might have been wrong to just walk away, but that's how I chose to do it. I didn't care to see you again, and I don't care to now." Again he started to mount.

"Afterward, I saw what you had to do, and I admit I ordered you to do too much, but what you did wasn't a mistake. I don't care how young those boys were, they all carried guns that packed death, and they knew how to use them. The law needs men like you. You were too good a man to lose then, and you're too good a man for me to let you slip away again without having a chance to talk you into coming back. It's a nasty profession sometimes, but somebody has to do it."

"*I* don't *have* to do it, and I won't again. Save your breath."

"Jim, it's just Brownie. You never got the chance to stop him before, but now you have. This was just a bad case, Jim. The rest would be easy after this job."

"You don't know what you're talking about," Whip said. "I've had several chances to stop Brownie. In fact, the first time I walked into his camp twelve years ago, I chose not to pull the trigger when I had the drop on him. When all the shooting was over, Brownie stood six feet from me with a loaded pistol and laughed at my empty one. He didn't shoot, John. He said, 'I owe you this. You could have killed me.' He holstered his gun and let me live when he could have easily done differently. When I came to this country, I purposely fought every man with my bare hands and I never had to kill a one. I've left that cursed iron hang from my saddle horn for ten years, and never needed it in order to live."

"Killing Brownie was necessary, Jim. You have to admit that. Sometimes a man has to kill."

Whip gazed off toward the tip of a snowy peak that glistened even in the darkness. He pointed to it.

"See that peak over there?" he asked.

"Yeah," Wilhelm answered.

"Well, someday I'm gonna ride this blue horse right up on the sharpest part of it." Whip turned and pointed south. "See that mountain range trying to hide out there in the darkness? Well, someday soon I'm gonna ride every hump on that mountain on this big blue horse."

"What are you saying, Jim?"

"I'm saying there's too much living to be lived for me to spend my life living to kill."

Whip untied the leather thong that held his holster snug to his leg. He unbuckled the belt, removed it from his hips, and then rebuckled it. He hung it over his saddle horn. The sore-footed blue dog came up to him from out of the darkness, and Whip stooped down and picked him up in his arms and set the dog in the saddle. He gathered up his hackamore rope and coiled it slowly.

"If my life's worth anything to you, John, forget

you saw me alive," he said. He stepped into the stirrup, mounted, and wrapped the long rope around the horn. He juggled the dog until he could sit down in the seat.

"Good-bye, John Wilhelm," Whip said softly. He turned Bandit Blue and immediately put the big horse into a slow lope. The black and the packhorse jumped into an easy canter behind him.

Onlookers saw the darkness swallow the horses and the rider, and for many moments afterward, they heard hooves pounding into the night. Then all was quiet. Jasper was the first to speak as Jessica and Mrs. Valez came up to him.

"I never knew a man could be that fast with a gun," he said.

"Neither did Brownie," Wilhelm said as he stepped up on the boardwalk. "Where's that cowardly excuse for a lawman you've got around here? Didn't he hear the shots?"

"He's probably scared that Brownie shot somebody, and he doesn't want to investigate it," Jasper grumbled.

"Mr. Ty is dead?" Mrs. Valez asked fearfully.

"Naw, I don't think that's the pardner Whip was talking about. Must have been something from years back," Jasper said.

"No, Father," Jessica murmured. "Whip is hurt something awful. It just seeped from him. Couldn't you feel it? He was different, really different."

"I'll say he was different," Jasper said. "So his

name's Jim Cordeen, not Whip, huh?" He looked at Wilhelm.

Wilhelm chewed his lip, deep in thought. Then he looked at the dark form of Brownie, still lying in the street, where curious onlookers tried to see who it was. He turned to Jasper.

"Jim? Jim who? If you're talking about a marshal who got killed about twelve years ago, no, that man's dead. If Whip Cordeen's your neighbor, Jasper Hunt, I can tell you you'll never have a better one." Wilhelm looked up and down the street, and then yelled so loud that those close to him covered their ears with their hands: "Reams! Get out here! Brownie's dead!"

Footsteps sounded on the boardwalk. Then, suddenly, Reams came striding into view.

"You didn't have to holler. I was on my way."

"I'll bet," Wilhelm mumbled sourly. He extended his hand to Jasper. "Well, this is good-bye. Whip kinda made my job easy. Hope I can get out this way when it's not business. Good-bye, pretty Jessica, and thanks for all your gracious hospitality, Mrs. Valez." He tipped his hat, turned, and disappeared into the night.

Reams edged up to the body of the outlaw and poked it gently with his foot, as if hesitant to anger it. Assured that the outlaw he feared was dead, he soon gave enough orders to maneuver a military troop. Brownie's body was removed from the middle of the street and toted down to the undertaker. Reams came over to Jasper and the women.

"I guess the laugh's on me," he said. "They said Whip Cordeen was faster than greased lightning, and when I look back and remember taking it upon myself to tell him about shooting a pistol, I feel pretty stupid."

"Keep feeling that way," Jasper snapped. "Maybe you'll get disgusted with yourself and resign."

Reams sobered, and Jasper rudely turned his back and ushered Jessica and Tina down the boardwalk. Minutes later they squeezed into the seat of the buggy. Jasper clucked to the horse and sent it into a fast trot toward home.

Morning sun warmed the ranch, bathing it in golden sunlight, but there was no brightness to the dismal scene that greeted Jasper as he drove the buggy into the yard. His men were gathered by the porch. Some hung their heads across folded arms, and others were staring at something near their feet as he drove up. Not a man did more than glance at Jasper. He could feel the bad news. He stepped down from the buggy and searched the group carefully. Many of his men were not there.

"What happened?" he asked.

"Nine won't be branding next spring, boss," a nearby cowboy muttered. "Old Rowdy didn't make it, and most of us have lost a pardner and all of us good friends. The outlaws got wiped out, but the price was too high."

Jasper removed his hat and ran his fingers

through his gray hair, his face stricken with sadness. His men were like his sons. He glanced up at the cowboy.

"What about Ty Holden?" he asked hesitantly.

"Ty makes ten, boss. You were lucky you didn't have to see Whip Cordeen. That tore my guts out. I reckon most of us got wet eyes for Whip as well as for those we put to sleep in the earth."

Jessica had stepped down from the buggy with Tina. She put her hands over her mouth, shut her eyes, and shuddered.

"Poor Mr. Whip," Tina moaned.

"I don't want him to be alone," Jessica whispered. "I'll go see if I can find him."

"No," Jasper said. "Whip will work it out himself. You let him be until he comes to us. Your company wouldn't replace Ty's at the moment, and you'd be infringing on Whip's privacy."

CHAPTER TEN

WHIP rode through the night and arrived at his small spread at dawn. He turned the three horses into the corral, made sure the water in the trough was full, then opened the gate to the fenced pasture so they could come and go as they pleased.

The solitude echoed around him. Whip imagined the constant jabbering if Ty had ridden into the yard with him. He studied the mound of ruins where the cabin had been. Suddenly he felt a desire to leave, to just strike out in any direction that would be away from where he stood there alone in the darkness. The magnitude of the silence left him feeling hollow within. He forced away the mood and looked around for his dog.

Heck had left to find Cat the minute he realized they were on home ground. The dog sniffed every nook and cranny, his stumpy tail wiggling excitedly while he bounced from spot to spot. A banana moon, a true rustler's moon, dimly lit the yard.

Whip carried the gear and panniers to the tack shed, then stepped out into the night again with the coat that Ty had lent him. He snugged it around his body and nestled down against the base of a cedar tree a hundred feet from the corrals. Though tired beyond tired, he found it impossible to sleep. Fond memories of his jabbering partner flooded his mind for hours, making him feel even more alone.

Suddenly, something zipped through the tall grass. A wild bundle of black and white fur leaped onto the coat, and then a purring and contented cat snuggled its way under the wrap of the coat and forced itself against the warmth of Whip's chest. The usually aloof tomcat mewed softly and rubbed the side of its face against Whip's shirt. The cat curled up as if its strange actions were normal and purred its way into a peaceful sleep.

Heck was still searching for the cat among the remains of the cabin. The thought of rebuilding it didn't excite Whip, and yet it had to be done. Searching for a way to get Ty off his mind, Whip recalled their arguments over the rebuilding of the cabin. Now he could see the value of Ty's suggestions that he had previously turned down, and he began to made plans for the rebuilding.

It was in the promising glow of dawn that Heck suddenly came loping up to Whip. He had not yet found the comfort of sleep and was watching for the sunrise. The dog sniffed the coat, wagged his tail, then growled and looked off into the cedars. The hair stood up all the way down his back.

Whip had carried the carbine with him to the tree where he had spent the night, and immediately he snatched it up. He shed the coat and sat up, studying the shadows and balancing the carbine in the crook of his arm.

Heck saw the cat as it hissed and slinked toward the tree trunk from the protection of the coat. The dog allowed the cat time to start up the tree, then leaped as if trying to catch it. Abruptly, Heck lost interest and gazed off into the trees, growling loudly.

Whip saw the Ute as he walked toward him several hundred feet out in the cedars. The Ute led his pony and walked slowly. He studied the rifle in Whip's hands, but didn't hesitate in his advance. Fifty feet away, he tied his mount, dragged a long blanket from a bundle on the horse's back, and pulled it around him as he settled down against the trunk of a cedar. After a look at Whip, he closed his eyes and went to sleep as the morning sun peeped over the eastern horizon.

As the sun warmed Whip's body, total fatigue took over. He watched the Ute for as long as he could, then gave in to a need for deep slumber.

The sun was high when he was awakened by Heck's growl. The dog had his lips drawn back, exposing his canines, and had his ears tucked in against his neck. Chasing off his drowsiness, Whip saw that the Ute was only a dozen feet away and standing with his arms folded, staring at him. They watched each other for several minutes. Then, instead of using sign language, the Ute spoke:

"A man who values my life, values his own. I stay."

The Ute turned with that announcement, and went to his pony and mounted. He reined the horse around and melted into the denseness of the cedar growth.

Whip intended to get to his feet and do some work during what was left of the day, but he lingered where he sat and let sleep overcome him again. He slept until just before evening, then again awoke at Heck's growl.

The Ute had hung two long strips of venison loin across a low-hanging limb. He gazed at Whip mutely, then turned his horse and rode away.

This time Whip forced himself into action and got to his feet. He looked off into the trees where the Indian had vanished from view, then walked over and pulled the loin from the limb. He made his way to the cellar and took the meat down into its coolness. Now he needed cooking utensils, and he left the cellar and walked over to the ruins of the cabin. He dug around in the ashes and located the iron skillet and the Dutch oven, which had both survived the fire. The coffeepot must have melted, because he found no part of it. The stove seemed in fairly good shape, but it lacked a pipe.

Whip continued to dig through the ashes, but came up with nothing salvageable. He went over to the fireplace and removed the loose rock. Inside, as safe as buried treasure, his money lay unharmed. He replaced the rock without removing the money, and spent a few more minutes probing the remains. Suddenly he remembered the supplies that were in the panniers that Brownie had filled in Magpie Springs.

The packs produced a coffeepot, utensils, coffee, and many other necessities. Fifteen minutes later Whip had a fire going in the fireplace and a pot of coffee hung from an iron hook imbedded in the masonry. He peeled potatoes that had been in the cellar and put them into a stew of meat. He scraped out an area large enough to walk around in near the fireplace and put down a big stump to sit on. The food was nearly done when Heck growled.

Whip saw the Ute dismount near the corral. The Indian tied his pony, then approached the ruins of the cabin in the dusk. He hesitated as his eyes took in the situation. Then he went to the woodpile, secured a stump for himself, and carried it through the ashes and set it down several feet from the one Whip was sitting on. The Ute sat, arms folded, and gazed from the stew pot to Whip.

"Eat," he said, then looked back into the fire.

"Coffee?" Whip asked.

"Coffee," the Ute answered, nodding.

Whip filled a cup and handed it to the Indian. He remembered what the Ute had said earlier—"I stay."

"I work hard," Whip said, studying the Indian.

"I help hard," the Indian answered, watching the flames.

Whip filled a couple of makeshift utensils with

stew and realized that he suddenly felt much better. No man took another's place when it came to a friendship, but a man could always accept new friendships. They only added to the abundance of life.

After a night of sound sleep Whip began the new day with an obsession to put the cabin up as quickly as he could. First he and the silent Ute cleared out the rubble left from the fire, which took all of the first day. On the second day they began cutting and sliding logs down from the timber above Whip's fenced pasture. By noon they had worn out the saddle horses, and Whip made a trip to the Irishman's and borrowed a team of drafts. From then on, the work went quicker. Nine days later the roof went on.

Somehow, between sessions of cabin construction, Whip found time to ride the horse that Jessica had described as a "magnificent prancing black." He found Brownie's mount to be a willing and obedient animal. He tested the horse's solidness time after time, and was totally satisfied with the beautiful beast's reliability.

In the meantime, something had happened that amazed Whip. Heck had spent a lifetime chasing Cat. Since their return, Heck still pursued Cat, but made it a point never to put enough effort into the chase to get his teeth into the cat.

Whip spent many moments watching the dog and cat come to a kind of truce. However, there was no truce between Cat and the Indian. Whip had a fear that if Cat didn't stop attacking the Ute, it was going to disappear mysteriously.

Whip was amazed at the sharpness of the Indian's mind. Whip never taught him a thing, verbally. The man would watch him for only moments, then suddenly put his hands to work and do exactly what Whip did. There was a kind of proud carriage about the Indian, no matter what the work called for.

The Indian never slept inside the cabin, even though he'd worked beside Whip to build it. That suited Whip fine, because he had used all his saddle blankets to make enough padding for one bed, let alone two. One morning about two weeks after Whip had shot Brownie in Magpie Springs, the Ute appeared inside the new cabin as the aroma of coffee drifted out the front window.

Whip had gotten several sections of stove pipe from the Irishman, and a few other store-bought objects that made it more than livable inside. In fact, the Irishman's wife had given him a quilt when he returned the draft horses.

The Indian sat down at the table and waited for Whip to fill the coffee cups. Whip delayed purposely, because they had been sharing jobs and he didn't intend to continue his habit of waiting on the Indian.

"Coffee," the Ute said after a while.

Whip pointed to the pot and the cups. "You," he said, then went back to cooking strips of venison.

Immediately, the Indian poured himself a cup and returned the pot. Whip turned away from the stove, gently caught the Ute by the arm, and pointed to his empty cup on the table.

"For me, you pour," he said.

"I'm no squaw," the Ute said, raising his chin arrogantly.

"Me, neither," Whip said, and continued to cook breakfast.

It took a few minutes for the Indian to mull this situation around in his mind. Then, suddenly, he picked up the coffeepot and poured Whip a cup. The Indian sat down and eyed Whip. Later, after breakfast, Whip pointed to the wash pan.

"You wash," he said.

"I'm no squaw," the Ute protested again.

"Me, neither," Whip repeated, then calmly whittled a toothpick.

The Ute stubbornly refused to move on that one, and he whittled himself a toothpick too. He stuck it in his mouth the same as Whip did and cast a proud eye on Whip.

"Do you know what a partner is?" Whip asked.

The Ute nodded.

"Well, if two men ride together, eat together, get mad together, and laugh together, they share the work together. This here job is half yours and half mine. I've been doing your work for two weeks. Today you start doing your half."

"No," the Ute said.

"Well, I ain't gonna do it all," Whip told him.

"I get a squaw, you get a squaw," the Ute suggested.

Whip almost choked. He stared at the Indian. Whip didn't regard a woman as someone to cook meals and do his cabin chores. More precisely, he thought of a woman as a cherished being whom a man loved and shared a life with. It seemed that the Ute thought her a means of avoiding undignified chores.

"If you eat in the cabin, you do the cabin work, the same as I do. If you don't share in the work, you eat outside in the blasted rain and snow!" Whip said.

He immediately got up and gathered up the dirty utensils. He put them in the wash pan and poured hot water over them. Before he could return the hot kettle of water to the stove, the Ute got to his feet and went to the wash pan. He poured in cold water from the bucket until he could put his hands in it, then set about scrubbing the utensils. Whip grabbed a towel and dried. Suddenly the Indian looked at Whip and grinned.

"Not so bad," he said.

"No," Whip mumbled, grinning, "not so bad. What's your name?"

"In white men's words, Wise Man Who Talks to the Moon."

"Well, Solomon, that's too long a title," Whip muttered.

"What's Solomon?" the Ute asked.

"A wise man."

"Solomon good name," the Ute said.

Much later in the morning, Whip drove the horses out of the pasture and into the corral. He caught up Bandit Blue and saddled him, then left him to warm up while he chopped wood. Just before noon, Solomon tapped Whip on the shoulder and then pointed to a spiraling cloud of dust to the south.

Whip studied the dust in the valley for a few minutes, then made out the familiar scene of Jasper's riders driving horses to his spread. After opening the large corral gate, he and Solomon crawled up on the fence and waited to see what was in the wind.

The herd swarmed over the brow of the hill, hazed on each side by Jasper's riders, and within minutes, Whip closed the gate on about thirty head of horses, most of them with saddles on their backs. Jasper rode up to Whip with Jessica at his side.

The sight of Jessica caused a struggle inside Whip. He had to force himself to stop looking at her, and in polite respect, he put all his attention on Jasper Hunt.

"Reckon saddled horses is odd, Jasper," he said.

"Well, these here mounts belonged to Brownie's gang, who are down saying hello to Satan. When they came wandering into my corrals, I remembered that you had been relieved of thirty-four head. There aren't that many, but they come with gear—that ought to help reimburse you for your loss. Those five horses without saddles are mine.

They're too hotheaded for my outfit. I brought them up to sell to you."

Whip found himself listening to Jasper, but gazing at Jessica again. When he realized it, he looked away.

"Twenty dollars a head," Whip said.

"Cripes! I paid seventy for them. You paid me twenty-five for the mustangs I sent to you!"

"Twenty or chase them home, Jasper."

The rancher glared at the broncobuster for a moment. Then, slowly, a warm smile spread across his face.

"Only because you're my neighbor," Jasper said. He nodded toward Solomon. "Didn't I see him riding with Brownie?"

"Reckon you did, but he rides with me now."

"He's a renegade Ute," Jasper growled.

"And his name's Solomon," Whip said, and dismissed Jasper's protest of his new partner. "Come on into the cabin and I'll pay you. You can write out a bill of sale."

When Jasper and Whip emerged from the cabin, Jessica was in the corral, mounted on Bandit Blue. She rode around at a walk, saw Whip coming down to the corrals, and pulled the horse to a stop when he came in through the gate.

"I need to separate some of the horses," he said. "Step down."

Whip helped her to dismount, then gathered Bandit Blue's reins and mounted. Jessica stepped back, and Whip nudged the roan with his spur. The horse shook its head and balked. Whip nudged the horse again, but Bandit Blue refused, tossing his head and pinning his ears to his neck.

If Whip hadn't had the audience, he might not have gotten firm with the roan, but the horse was causing him a little embarrassment. He pulled a rein to turn the horse slightly, then poked him a little hard with his heel. Bandit Blue exploded.

Whip gritted his teeth and sailed on high, a skillful rider who seldom lost his seat. But instead of jamming back to earth, the roan spun halfway around, then turned his belly up and began his descent. Whip knew the horse wouldn't land on his back, but somehow he gave in to the desire to lean sideways, in case the horse didn't turn back over on his legs.

Bandit Blue flipped back with his right side up, and hit the ground with a solid jar. Whip was leaning over, and the impact had its effect. He was shaken loose, and when the horse swooped down low and sideways to the ground, he lost his secure seat. Bandit Blue launched himself into the heavens, bawled like a mad bull, then went into a spin and left Whip somewhere in the atmosphere, unhorsed.

The dust poofed, then began to sift and settle as Whip rose to his knees from the corral dirt. He looked around and stood up, swaying unsteadily. He put a wicked eye on the blue hide that stood calmly near Jessica, licking her outstretched palm with his silky pink tongue.

Whip stalked over to the horse, stepped around Jessica, and, almost angrily, began to jerk loose the cinch. He pulled off the saddle with one sweep and threw it down on the ground near the fence. He left the corral, but soon returned with the saddle from Jessica's horse. He saddled Bandit Blue, left the corral, and then led Jessica's mount into the big corral and turned it loose. Next, he caught up the flashy black and led it into the corral where Jessica stood holding Bandit Blue, unsure of what was happening. Jasper and his cowboys looked on, watching Whip curiously.

Whip saddled the black, then traded headstalls with Bandit Blue. He seemed to be steaming down slowly, and by the time he had the black saddled, a lot of the fire had left his eyes. He turned to Jessica and said, "Take that worthless blue hide home with you. He belongs to you now, by his own choice."

"Oh, Whip, I can't," she protested. "He's yours."

"He only tolerated me, Jessica. First he took up with my dog, now he's taken up with my girl."

"*Your girl!*" Jessica repeated in a strange tone.

Whip felt a red glow steal across his face. He had not intended to say that. It had just slipped out. He ventured a quick glance up at the line of cowboys and Jasper Hunt, all perched speechlessly along the top rail, a shocked expression on every face except Solomon's. Whip pulled his hat down as low as possible. He had intended to sort horses, but now, due to the awkward position that his careless tongue had put him in, it had become imperative that he disappear fast. Swinging aboard the black, he muttered to Jasper as he started out the gate, "See you later."

"Hey, hold on! I want a discussion with you," Jasper hollered.

"Talk to my pardner!" Whip hollered back as he loped the black toward the open country.

Jessica stared after him for several moments; then his words really struck home. She immediately stepped into the stirrup and swung into the saddle. She put Bandit Blue into a dead run at the corral gate and thundered after Whip.

"How come that contrary horse lets her ride?" one of the cowboys questioned in a baffled tone.

"The blue horse belonged to a white woman in Kansas," Solomon said.

"How do you know?" the cowboy asked.

Solomon responded with a smile and a proud lift of his chin. "Good," he said. "Whip buy squaw." He nodded approvingly and folded his arms across his chest.

"What are you talking about?" Jasper growled.

"Whip traded the roan horse for the squaw," Solomon answered, putting a knowing eye on Jasper.

"White men don't buy women."

"Whip's squaw," Solomon said stubbornly. He reached out and put a strong grip on Jasper's arm. "You drink coffee?"

The question sounded like an order to Jasper, and he didn't want to offend Whip's new partner.

"Sure, I'll have a cup of coffee," he said.

"Good. I'll pour, you wash."

The fleet black was nearly at the river before Bandit Blue began to close the gap between them. Whip turned in the saddle, suddenly aware of the running horse behind him. He pulled the black to a stop and waited for Jessica to ride up.

She slid the blue roan to a stop barely yards from him, then walked the roan up beside the black. Whip avoided her eyes at first. He was upset that his dreams had voiced themselves so unceremoniously.

"I reckon I embarrassed you, Jessica. I apologize for what happened," he said.

"It surprised me more than anything else."

"I guess I'm not too old to be a fool sometimes," he muttered.

"You're not old, Whip."

He shot an intent look at her, wondering why the age thing was coming up again. He knew where he stood, so why was she arguing about it?

"I guess I'm too young for you to have meant what you said back there," she said, fiddling with her reins.

"Too young? That's not the problem. The problem is that I'm too old for you."

"No, I'm too young for you, and that's why you weren't serious a minute ago. You said something you didn't mean, so you had to run away. I misunderstood and thought maybe you might have meant it, so I followed you. But I see that I'm just bothering you."

Jessica couldn't help the disappointed look that crossed her face. Dejectedly, she turned her horse. But the look on her face fairly burned into Whip, and he reached out and grabbed Bandit Blue's reins.

"Jessica," he said softly, "there's never a time when a woman's too young for a man, but there is a time when a man is too old for a woman. I thought you'd have your hat set for a young puncher, not an old broncobuster."

"You're not old, Whip."

"If you believe that, then I'll tell you that I meant what I said back there, even though I didn't plan to say it."

A tear mingled with her smile as she put her dancing blue eyes on Whip. Bashfully, she looked out across the river.

"Get down and let's talk," he said softly.

Whip held Bandit Blue and gave her a hand down. Then he led both horses over to a tree and tied them. He walked back to Jessica and took her by the arm. They walked down to the river's edge and watched the rapids for a few minutes.

Whip reached into his shirt pocket and removed something, but he kept it clutched in his fist. She looked curiously from his hand to his face.

"What is that?" she asked.

He took hold of her hand and turned the palm upward. Slowly, he lowered his clutched fist into hers and opened his fingers. A gold engraved watch slipped into her hand.

Jessica struggled against the tears of joy that blurred her sight. She wrapped her fingers around the watch and drew it to her breast, closing her eyes.

"Mother, I have it," she whispered.

She looked at Whip and wiped the tears from her eyes, then placed the watch carefully into her skirt pocket.

"I don't mean to be a silly crybaby. It just meant so much to Mother and me," she said.

"Feelings aren't silly, Jessica." Whip put an arm round her shoulders and pulled her close to him. They began to stroll along the riverbank. "Is this all right with you?"

"Your arm?" she asked.

"Yes, holding you close like this."

She was quiet for a moment, then laid her head against him, swinging in rhythm with his footsteps as they ambled along the grassy bank.

"I like it, Whip. It makes me feel warm and safe."

"Safe from what?" he asked.

"I don't know from what. Just warm and safe."

Whip stopped, grasped her shoulders, then gently turned her to face him. She looked up at him with a look that made his heart leap happily. He put his arms around her and pulled her to him, gently resting his chin on her head as they both felt the glow that promised a beautiful love was being born.

"I hate walking, Jessica," he whispered. "How about sitting on the bank over there by the river?"

Hands clasped, they walked over to the grassy bank. They sat down side by side with their feet hanging over the water.

"I can't take Bandit Blue from you," Jessica said.

"Why not? He doesn't like me one bit."

"But I can't pay you for him. Maybe Father can, but I don't have any money."

"You've already paid me in dreams," he said quietly, and he tossed a pebble into the dark waters.

Jessica watched the water for a bit, then turned and looked at him with a grin tucked in between matching dimples.

"Tell me the dream," she said.

Whip took a deep breath and tossed in another pebble. He turned his face toward her, leaned over, and gently placed a kiss on her lips.

"That's one, and there's many more."

Jessica laughed and blushed, then sobered. But a light lingered in her eyes, and it warmed Whip just like the sunlight upon her golden hair.

"Whip, you've never apologized for stealing those kisses," she said.

"Well, darling, you got in a couple of real stinging slaps for that, and I figure we're even on that score."

Suddenly he leaned over again, only inches from her lips, and boldly studied her eyes. Then he kissed her softly again.

"We're not even anymore," he whispered.

Jessica leaned forward and kissed him lightly.

"Now we are," she said.

"Tell me, Jessica, would you spend a lifetime with a man who didn't like to stay even?"

"I wouldn't want to spend a lifetime with one who did," she answered.

Whip took her in his arms and let his eyes travel over her beautiful face. The love of this woman had been a teasing thing that he had only dared to dream in his loneliness. She looked back at him, and the look beckoned, waiting for him to keep the score uneven. Answering that beckoning call, Whip kissed her tenderly, beginning at last to live the dreams that he had dared to dream.